The Flip Side of the Bottle

By Tanya Lee Cote

All rights reserved. No part of this publication may be reproduced, stored or transmitted in any form or by any means, electronic, mechanical, photocopying, recording, scanning, or otherwise without written permission from the publisher. It is illegal to copy this book, post it to a website, or distribute it by any other means without permission.

Tanya Lee Cote has no responsibility for the persistence or accuracy of URLs for external or third-party Internet Websites referred to in this publication and does not guarantee that any content on such Websites is, or will remain, accurate or appropriate.

Designations used by companies to distinguish their products are often claimed as trademarks. All brand names and product names used in this book and on its cover are trade names, service marks, trademarks and registered trademarks of their respective owners. The publishers and the book are not associated with any product or vendor mentioned in this book. None of the companies referenced within the book have endorsed the book.

This novel is a work of Fiction. Some elements are based on a true story. In all cases, characters names have been changed to protect the privacy and identity of individuals. Certain characters may be composites, or entirely fictitious. Timelines and places have been changed for dramatic purposes. This book is not intended to be a substitute for the medical advice of a licensed physician. The reader should consult with their doctor in any matters relating to his/her health

Collaborators
Marc Bureau- cover artist
Mead's Editing LLC- Editor

Copyright © 2018 Tanya Lee Cote, All rights reserved.
ISBN-13: 978-1-9995559-1-7

DEDICATION

I dedicate this book to my mother, who loved me the best she knew how. I thank her for providing me with so much contrast in my life that I know where I've been and where I want to go.
To my brother, whose love I could not go without and whose pain I recognize all too well . . . I see you.
To my nanou, uncle, and cousin, all of whom have been a lifeline—I thank you for loving me.
To my husband, for our insatiable desire to be better people, for how far we have come, and for the moments in between. Thank you for being you. Thank you for allowing me to learn how to love.
To my children, who make me take a hard look at myself, who help mama find the courage within herself to heal. My beautiful babies, thank you for choosing me to be your mama.
For myself . . .

CHAPTER 1

It was her shriek that woke me that night. Although we were in the same apartment, those thin walls separated my world from hers. I couldn't tell how long they'd been fighting, but I knew he was drunk . . . whatever drunk meant. He was always drinking. It made him mean. It made her small. I could hear him slurring as the words escaped his mouth.

"You're gonna let me fuck you, like the bitch you are. You're mine, you whore."

I didn't know what the words he spoke meant, but I knew they were dirty. The way he said them made me quiver. I could smell the booze in his voice, as though he were breathing right over me. I could taste the putrid words he spat.

And then, like a crash after the silent gap between thunder and lighting, I heard the blow. The impact of his fist on her body resonated throughout the house like the echo of a yodeler across the mountains.

She let out a low whimper. "You get off of me! Get off! I said no, you son of a bitch!"

She always sounded so strong—fierce, even. Her five-foot-four petite frame did not do justice to her immense ferocity. She was stoic—often meeting his brutality with mere indifference—but when he overpowered her, her voice almost sounded like mine: trifling. Scared.

I curled myself up into a ball as small as my five-year-old body could make. I shivered. The house was chilly; my worn bed sheets barely kept the cold at bay. I could feel the struggle that was happening in her room. It vibrated into my body, seizing me. I closed my eyes tightly. Nights like these occurred often—most times it didn't last too long. I didn't know how she would get it to stop, but it always did.

Tonight, though, it was different. The chaos seemed to go on for much longer, and she sounded weak. I believe this night was the first time I ever said a prayer. I didn't know who could possibly hear me or save us, but I kept repeating: *Please, please, please make him stop. Please, please, please make him stop.* And then, as clear as the darkness that surrounded me, I heard a voice.

Go and save her. Go now.

I obeyed. Obedience was ingrained into every cell of my being. I sat up in my bed and felt the courage of a lioness invade my little body. My pink nightgown, barely long enough to cover my knees, made me feel exposed. No amount of heat could make those concrete floors warm, especially on nights like tonight. I shivered as my feet touched the ground. I pushed aside the bed sheet that hung across my doorframe, serving as a makeshift door, and crept over to her room.

Silently, I tried the knob. It turned and I entered. I was immediately blinded by the brightness of the room; my eyes squinted to adjust. I had walked onto a stage where white lights were illuminating a violent scene. Everything seemed so bright in contrast to her. She was red, black, and blue. I could taste the blood spilling from her mouth. I could see the bloodstains dotting her nightgown. The crimson liquid had dripped down her body and was drying around her ankles. It was everywhere.

I could feel her pain—her fear.

He never saw me, but she did. Her pupils dilated. She feared for me. I could already read her mind by then.

"Sophie! Get out of here!" The urgency in her eyes was alarming. For a moment, I almost listened. The drumming of my heartbeat was deafening. But I had a mission—and relentless determination to complete it.

Before he could grab her, I snuck over to his side and clung to his dirty, bloodied arm. My little body gripped onto him like a fierce cub. My primal instinct took over as I bit into him with all the strength I had. My teeth bit down through his black arm hair, past his flesh, until I could feel his pulse. Until I could taste his anger.

"You little bitch, get the fuck off of me!" he growled, lifting up his forearm and swinging it violently. My body swung back and forth easily, as if he were shaking a rag doll.

I held on as long as I could, until he flung me with all his might. I lost my grip and flew through the air as though time had ceased to exist. Everything was silent and peaceful for a fraction of a moment. And then, with an abrupt halt, my body collided with the wall and fell to the ground. I gasped as the impact took my breath away. Although I could feel the throbbing in my shoulder and down my arm, none of that mattered. I raised myself to my knees and looked up at the face of pure hatred glaring down at me. Defiance flowing through my veins, I stared back into the eyes that had no contrast between pupil and iris.

I had succeeded. I had given her enough time to recover— a moment to catch her breath. That was all she needed, and with incredible strength and speed, she pushed him into the wall and ran to me. She knelt to the ground and lifted me up. Her face was so close to mine I could feel the heat from her body radiating like fire. I could see the different hues of green in her eyes. She held my gaze, silently pleading.

Then, she spoke in a whisper. "Go wake up your brother. Go now! You two go get the police."

With her hands lightly gripping my shoulders, she gently pushed me out of the room and gave me a final, resilient glance. I saw her take one deep inhale. Then, she slowly closed the door behind her, and just like that, with one solemn *click*, she returned to face him.

I got up from my knees and started across the living room, the soles of my feet sticking to the concrete floor as I ran through the kitchen and down the hallway to my brother's room. The six-hundred-square-foot apartment seemed to stretch for miles.

My destination was finally in reach. My body trembled. The thumping in my chest was so strong it felt as though my heart would protrude and fall to the ground.

I barged into my brothers' room. He was already awake and standing by his dresser. He looked at me and knew what we needed to do. This wasn't the first time he'd been required to be the savior. He was only ten years old, but if you peered into his eyes then, you would have seen the pain and turmoil of an old man. Anguish would forever be embedded in his soul.

He held his hand out to me. "Come on, put on your shoes. Hurry. Hold my hand now and run, okay?"

We looked at each other, our silence speaking volumes. Hand in hand, we opened the door to the coolness of the night, our breath dancing in front of us. Together we peered out into the dimly lit world, then we crossed the threshold and leapt, leaving behind the theatrical tragedy.

The sound of our little feet echoed through the crisp night air.

***

Her bruises had faded slightly. The black, blues, and purples had given way to the lighter hues of yellow, and she had begun to eat again. She stood at the stove, humming as she made our breakfast. We were feasting, and it wasn't even time for the Christmas hampers. She had a renewed hunger, a certain *joie de vivre,* as the French would say. My brother and I sat quietly watching the spectacle—her happiness was somewhat of an unusual sight in our household. She glowed when she wasn't drinking or around him. Many would say she had a great deal of potential.

Lucifer was still in jail—it had been two weeks. He was allowed out on bail, but no one had bailed him out this time. Life was almost joyous; her smile, intoxicating. She could make you believe anything was possible; during these times, my brother and I had hope.

Our little bodies sat as still as erect blades of grass on a windless day. We hoped this moment would last, but we knew we had to anchor ourselves for the eventual upturn of the wind.

***

"Sophie. Sophie, are you with me? How about you tell me how you felt when he wasn't around?" he asked. After a brief, searching pause, he continued to meddle. "How did that make you feel?"

He looked at me expectantly. I couldn't bring myself to speak. My throat was dry; the motion of swallowing was agonizing. The recollections were as difficult to recount as they had been to experience when they happened.

I took a deep breath in. "I-I'm not sure how I felt—I was five. I'm not there in my head yet. I just . . ." I rubbed my temples, gliding my hand over my eyes. I wanted to erase the visions behind them. "I just can't think of ways to verbalize this stuff to you any more than I just did. I know you want me to give you more—more details, more information, more emotions—but I just can't. Not right now." I kept my eyes on my lap, pretending to pick at some lint that had magically appeared.

This had been an enormous divulgence for me, but I was still a coward. I knew how it felt because I could still feel it resonating through every cell in my body. It was as real today as it had been then.

My façade appeared strong and resolved, but I was shattered. I knew he could see through me. I didn't like doing this to myself; the recollections placed me back into that five-year-old's body. I was still her: small, terrified, and already oh-so-damaged. Going back to that place made me lose my grip on reality, and the fear of losing control over what could happen to me was, well, inconceivable.

"Listen, we both know this is very challenging for you, and I appreciate the effort that you have put in today. But you agreed to fully involve yourself this time, right?" His eyes narrowed in on me. "I agreed to take you on again because I believe that you can heal. *But*—and this a big *but*—it's only by allowing yourself to express the trauma that you have endured in a safe environment that you can mend what needs to mend. Sophie, you do want that, right?"

He gazed at me, awaiting a reply; an acknowledgment of some sort, that of course he was right, and that yes, I had asked him to take me on again as his client.

I looked at him for a moment, tilting my head very slightly, as if a different angle could help me dislike him. Right now, I wanted to hate him, so I could give myself a reason to quit. Unable to find a valid reason to hate him, I found the next best thing.

He would become a victim of my wrath.

"Maybe one day I want to reach that beautiful fantasy of a happy, healthy woman, with the healthy relationships that you're describing, Paul. But for now, I can't even stand my own fuckin' reflection, or the thoughts in my head. I don't know how to be an adult. I don't even know if happiness is an actual feeling, or if its just a made-up emotion that people proclaim exists to make themselves feei better about the mediocracy of their own existence. Maybe everyone is just *faking it*. Because I sure as shit have never felt happiness for longer than a moment at a time. It's always so fleeting. Maybe it's not even an achievable goal for me to reach for—happy, healthy—let alone trying to love someone else when I don't even have love for myself! I'm just trying to survive here!" I exhaled loudly.

He flinched as the words I spoke shot at him like daggers. If I was good at one thing, it was reading people. I moved uneasily in my chair.

"Ah fuck, I'm sorry. Listen, Paul, this was lovely and all, but I have to get to work." I glanced at my phone. It was still early for work, but the time was my scapegoat.

I grabbed my jacket, forced a polite smile, and kept my eyes to the ground. I didn't want to look at him anymore. He was a handsome man. His salt-and-pepper hair and deep brown eyes made him easy on the eyes. He seemed genuinely empathetic. I liked him. Well, I both hated and liked him, you know?

In a soft tone, he said, "You're doing phenomenal, Sophie. Give yourself time to heal. It's very challenging and demanding on yourself to express the trauma you've been through. Try to be gentle with yourself. I'll see you in a couple of weeks."

He politely walked me to the door. As I exited, he placed his hand on my shoulder and gave it a light squeeze. There was something I found both amusing and repulsive about doctors, therapists, and the gesture of the shoulder squeeze. I wondered if it was something they were taught in school. I could just imagine a professor instructing aspiring health professionals: *Hey, guys, don't forget to do the shoulder squeeze, especially when you have a distraught client.* I figured it had to be a prerequisite to getting their degrees or something. Anyway, maybe one day I'd ask.

Regardless, he did care about my progress, but I just couldn't be where he thought I could or should be right now. Paul was the third psychologist I'd seen in the last year. Evidently, I was trying. It's not that I didn't want to do any of this; it's that I didn't want to *do* any of *this.* And of course, I just hadn't been able to connect with the others, but Paul was different. He was wise and insightful. He had the ability to coax the words out. He didn't make me feel any dirtier than I already felt, and he didn't make me feel violated when I spoke. He accepted my outbursts and fluctuating moods with ease. He guided me to speak. I knew I needed his help, so here I was—leaving.

***

The sharpness of the cold air was a relief. The stinging on my face took away from the vicious feelings inside. I pulled up the collar on my jacket and reached into my pocket. I found my cigarettes, pulled one out, and lit it. I took a big drag and felt an instant relief when the smoke enveloped my lungs. I watched what was happening around me: Cars rushed by on the concrete overpass, the people on the sidewalks scurried about like little zombies. The whole city felt gray; devoid of any pulse. I looked around for an ashtray to put out my smoke—none could be found.

"You've gotta be kidding me," I muttered.

The pollution in the air was thick and garbage blew around when the wind rose, so why would I give a fuck about contributing to it? I walked briskly to my car, taking two final puffs before reluctantly throwing my smoke to the ground. Annoyed, I searched through my pockets for my keys. After finally finding them, I sat down in my car, slamming the door behind me.

"What the fuck does that even mean, *you're doing phenomenal*?" I looked at myself in my rear-view mirror. My ice blue eyes narrowed. I moved a strand of my brown hair away from my face—a face that could be pretty if only it wasn't so rigid. I hated myself; I was filth. Incapable of staring at my reflection any longer, I put my car in gear and sped off to work.

As I pulled into the parking lot, I could see that there were cars lining each side of the building. *It's going to be a busy night*, I thought. *Showtime.*

I could hear Ginuwine's song "Pony" blaring through the speakers, so I knew it was still early enough that the second round of girls hadn't hit the stage yet. I pulled out my work bag and walked into the bar.

The smoke machine intertwined with the cigarette smoke. The drift from the door made the heavy cloud dance above the drunkards below, making the scene look somewhat mysterious and beautiful. The odor of men and booze, women and sex, was a sweetly repulsive and invasive mixture that comforted me. The dysfunction was normal—it was almost a requirement upon entry. I knew this world a little too well . . .

***

"Look Mom, I finished another one!" my excited voice rang out.

I had been sitting like a good girl all evening, engrossed in the drawings I had decided to create to sell to the clients at the bar. Knowing that my mother couldn't give me any money, because we never had any to spare, I had taken it upon myself to get what I wanted: candy.

Mom looked over at me, proud that I was such a well-behaved child. Maybe even a little entrepreneurial? "That's really good, Sophie." She smiled as she popped another cap off a bottle.

I went around the bar, hopping up on bar stools beside the customers, and sold my masterpieces for twenty-five cents each. Everyone looked at me and smiled and pinched my cheeks. They gave me extra money just because I was so darned cute, and they were all drunk. I loved it.

"Mom, I made five whole dollars!" I shouted with joy. "I'm going to the store and I'll be right back," I called as I ran out the door, not waiting for permission.

My mother never wondered or worried about me. Even at my young age, she knew I was responsible, capable, and aware of my surroundings. *Either that or she didn't give a shit.* I grew up in bars, never knowing that other kids didn't live the same way as I did. How boring their lives must have been…

***

I scanned the room. The regular drunks were slouched over their beers, cradling their bottles like infants while watching the women perform. Oh, the irony.

"Good evening, beautiful, in for a great night?" a voice shouted above the music. "I hope you packed a cute skirt in that bag. You know I've been asking you to wear one ever since you started working, yet you refuse to listen." He gave me a smile and a wink.

This one gesture seemed to be a prominent part of the night life, one that had many innuendos. The guys sure did like to wink—a lot. It was an *I wink, I own you* type of thing.

"You know, Frank, I told you I didn't wear skirts. There's enough pussy and flesh running around here, I don't need to be freezing mine off to make money," I laughed. I gave him a wink in return, along with my devious smile.

I didn't welcome authority, so I easily found ways to manipulate my way around it. I walked to him, wrapped my arm around his shoulder, and gave him a little squeeze. Then I pressed my cheek against his, embracing him with a very French-mannered kiss on either cheek, making sure that I made the loud obnoxious *moah* sounds.

The proximity made me seem less defiant. Although most knew I was a stubborn woman with an attitude problem, I had overcome my need to be obedient years ago. Now, I was constantly altering who I was so I could be whoever I needed to be in the moment. My mother called me a chameleon.

Right now, I was a lascivious badass—not the worst portrayal of myself I had to offer.

"Besides, the guys like cleansing their eyes every now and then on a woman who leaves something to the imagination. You see, I'm giving them the best of both worlds. I think that may warrant a raise . . ." I shrugged innocently, teasing him.

Frank laughed. “You conniving bitch. Always wanting more money for less.” He looked around at the guys seated in the surrounding tables and laughed harder. They reciprocated with a flawless, canned laughter. “What would I do without your smart-ass replies? Go upstairs and get ready for your shift, your bar needs to be open in thirty minutes.” He laughed yet again and turned his back, affirming his stance of superiority, silently stating that the conversation was now closed.

As I walked past the stage, one of the customers groped my ass. It wasn’t unusual behavior, nor was it frowned upon. It all depended on how much grabbing took place, how long it lasted, how much tolerance one had, and, well, it mostly depended on how much you were willing to play along. I turned and slapped his hand in a playful manner, giving him a coy smile. He seemed pleased with himself. He mumbled something inaudible that sounded very much like *I know you liked that.*

His eyes squinted as he gave me a grin. I reciprocated the meme mostly by obligation—there’s that famous adage: *Don’t bite the hand that feeds you.*

Sometimes I wished I could.

I hated being touched if I wasn’t the one calling the shots, but this was work and work meant money—lots of it. And that’s exactly why I put myself through all of this.

As I walked upstairs, I could hear the shuffling of feet getting ready. There was a constant frenzy of girls crossing the hallway from one changing room to the next. Some sported their stage outfits, others simply wandered around naked. I navigated my way through all the flesh to the back room which housed my locker.

I stripped myself of my street clothes and took out my work outfit: black, low-rise fitted pants, a black, laced crop top, and of course, my black, studded ankle boots—the type of stuff I wouldn't dare wear on the outside.

"Oh, Sophie. How are you? It's such a busy night, I really don't feel like putting up with any touchy-feely, dirty bastards tonight." Solange sighed and gave a look of exasperation as she rested her naked body against the makeup counter.

I looked up and gave her a genuine smile. "Hey, Solange! I'm doing *great*!" I over-exaggerated.

"Did you see that crowd already?" she asked with big eyes.

"I hear ya, there's lots of them tonight. What is happening? Is it like a holiday that I've forgotten about or what? Fuck, some days, I tell ya. Every time I want a quiet night, I get this." I rolled my eyes. We both giggled.

Solange was a sweet French girl from Montreal. She came in every Thursday to Saturday with the stripper bus. She was eighteen years young and dainty. The baby face of the show; the long blonde hair, big blue eyes type of girl. She usually indulged the innocent child and naughty schoolgirl fantasies.

I never had judgment toward any of these girls. The truth was, there wasn't much separating me from any of them. The only reason I wasn't up on one of those poles was my unforgivable cellulite and the size of my areolas; all those years my cousin had spent taunting them hadn't been in vain, after all.

I had a natural pull to be protective of Solange. She was fun and let herself be easily carried into all kinds of situations; maybe she was a little naïve. I worried that this life would get the best of her. One too many times, I had witnessed girls overdosing in the bathroom because of their lack of self discipline. It was a predicament I wanted her to avoid. I also suffered from a minor savior complex, so really, I couldn't help it. I often felt I *had* to save people.

I gave her a side squeeze. "I'll keep an eye out for you tonight, just try to take the booths closest to me, all right?" I placed my hands on her upper arms and held her at arm's length. I stared at her intently and resumed my little lecture. "Because its busy out there and Frank won't appreciate me wandering too far off when I do my rounds, let alone extra ones, 'kay?"

"You're the sweetest." She moved my hands out of the way, leaned her entire nakedness into me, and wrapped her arms around my neck, giving me a peck on the cheek. I reciprocated the hug.

There was nothing uncomfortable or sexual about this gesture, because to me, Solange was Solange and nothing more. She certainly wasn't Vicky; the first girl I ever slept with and the only girl I ever tried to love— *my attempt at love had been easier with her than with any man I had ever dated.*

My mind drifted back to our first time. Our bodies intertwined, our tongues ferociously tasting one another. The saltiness of her neck lingered in my mouth. Our bodies fused at the hips as I caressed her breasts, taking her entire bosoms in my hands. I held her tightly, teasing her erect nipples with my finger and thumb, gently rolling them between my fingers. Her mouth opened and she moaned. I pressed my lips against hers as she glided her hands in between my legs, where she was met by the warm, luscious wetness of my sex. In return, I pressed my body against hers as she made me plead for more. The ecstasy engulfed us, the thundering of the music beyond the bathroom door resonated as though we had teleported ourselves to a distant place . . .

Solange snapped her fingers. My mouth was dry, my dazed expression blankly staring at her petite frame. I hadn't noticed that she'd been talking.

I returned my attention to the sounds that were coming from her mouth. Finally, her words became audible again. She turned and lifted two outfits in front of me.

"So, which one?" With an impatient yet questioning expression on her face, she dangled two tiny pieces of fabric that made up the most minute of outfits.

I turned my head slightly and considered the options. "Umm, why don't you go with the ultra-pink tonight? It's gonna help you stand out. Not that you need it, though. You're a hottie," I winked at her.

She seemed pleased with my answer.

I walked out of the changing room, brushing off the recollection.

I headed to the managers office. He was the one that kept our 'first aid kit.' It basically consisted of a panoply of drugs, and I seriously wondered if they hid this stuff in the real first aid kit to fool people. And, did we actually *have* a real first aid kit? That was a legit question.

I opened the door. The manager was on the phone.

"I'm just in for my starter," I whispered.

He nodded. His severe expression made him impressively dismissive with the least amount of effort—just a slight gesture of the head.

I opened the metal case and filed through the ludicrous array of drugs the establishment kept available to us. I pondered my choices. A little bit of cocaine . . . nope, I never liked putting anything in my nose. Weed . . . nope, it made me sleepy and paranoid that I would die from oxygen deprivation. Then my eyes rested on my all-time favorite: Canadian speed. My drug of choice, *every time*.

I'd always suspected—more or less known—that the club had more substances available than what was in that box, but I chose not to ask about anything that did not directly affect me. The less information I had, the better. I still liked to believe that although I was drifting in this world, I could remain disassociated from it. It was typical of me to always be different from all those around. Irrespective of where I was and who I was with, *I always had to be different*.

I reached into the box and grabbed a couple of pills. I wasn't proud of it, but I *needed* them to last the entire night. I needed them so I could face this maladjusted reality with a conforming smile. Well, in all honesty, the only way I could handle being a doormat was by being high. I grabbed my baggy and showed the manager what I'd taken.

He raised his pen. *One moment.* Still holding the phone between his shoulder and his ear, he opened up *The Book* and jotted my withdrawal on his very organized spreadsheet: *Sophie +2*.

If I'd had the ability to cower to my own self-destructive behaviors, I would have. As much as I was appalled by my actions, I was equally capable of telling the righteous side of my brain to *SHUT UP*.

The manager gave me a thumbs-up, and I walked out of the office.

The music was hypnotizing, and the whirlwind of girls swaying and swooshing their bodies back and forth put everyone in a captivated trance—or maybe it was the smell of pussy juice that did that? Anyway, the atmosphere facilitated my job at the back bar, where all the men and a few girls sat mostly quiet, enjoying the show.

I made extra rounds to the stalls as promised.

The night proceeded quite smoothly, and despite the preconceived inkling Solange and I had shared earlier, nobody got groped by the nasty-dirty men.

I must admit this was what I would call a successful shift. The night wrapped up and I gathered my portion of the other bar's tips in addition to my stuff. I was pleased with the overall tally; this was exactly why I worked here.

I grabbed my bag and swapped my work shoes for my comfy pair. "Goodnight, y'all!" I shouted to the guys and girls who had all retreated upstairs.

"Night, Soph," a symphony replied.

I opened the door. A rush of wind swept over my body like a current cleansing my soul. I could see the first glimpse of daybreak. Everything was silent and all that remained was the subtle humming emitting from the speakers. The slight shimmer of the sun's golden rays peeked from the tops of the trees. I stood there for a moment, then reached into my pocket for my smokes and lit one. I inhaled deeply. I could feel the vibration within slowly subsiding.

"I made it to another day," I muttered to myself.

CHAPTER 2

I turned my car onto the road that would lead me home. Well, not exactly my home, but the home my mother and my stepfather rented from his aunt. Regardless of the technicalities, I called it *my* home and I felt proud of it. This was the first time in my life we had lived at the same place for longer than nine months. It may not seem like a big deal—people would sometimes say I should just be happy that at least I had a roof over my head, that we didn't live in a shelter or on the streets—but still, moving roughly twenty-plus times within my twenty-one years of existence . . . well, in my opinion, that's a whole lot of moving, and not something I could necessarily use as an asset on my resume. *Proficient in moving* didn't sound very good—unless, of course, I'd wanted to work for a moving company.

On top of that, I came to understand that it didn't give me the sense of stability a child should experience; it's not like we were moving around to see the wonders of the world. Anyway, this house didn't consist of a mediocre apartment complex, or even an old dilapidated house. We'd been down the dilapidated house route many times before, because my mother loved projects. Even though she never fully saw them through, she kept wanting to fix things—as though it would somehow rectify the self-sabotage and lack of control she had over her own life. If she failed to fix the wounds created by the invisible battles she fought within (which, may I add, she never successfully vanquished), she would abandon her projects mid-way and set us off on a quest for a new battlefield, where she would again attempt to conquer the fictitious assailants.

In other words, she would skip out on rent a time too many and leave before the landlord kicked us out. She called it *being proactive*.

Who knows—I wasn't a shrink, just a casualty of her self-destructive behaviors. Like a co-pilot who's obligated to sit for the ride knowing very well that the captain is a shitty flier, I sat along for my mother's disastrous flight. All because of what . . . moral obligation?

For once, looking at our current dwelling, no one could visibly see that we were the poor folks—a sub-par category of society.

***

The narrow road twisted and turned as I sped under the tree-covered lane. The low-lying branches rustled as I drove by. I watched them swaying in my rear-view mirror. I slowed down as I reached the fork in the road, making a slight right. As I came up to the first lake on my left, I slowed and rolled my window down. The fresh sent of foliage and water enticed my senses and for a moment, I was reinvigorated. I imagined my enzymes slowly extenuating the last remaining metabolites of the drugs I had consumed the night before. The pleasant sensation this natural environment produced could never be recreated by any artificial drug, no matter how amazing the high was.

I slowly accelerated, continuing my way home. A few meters down, I reached the last house on the road, and the second lake. I pulled up to the house. The bare, weather-worn, wooden planks of the exterior were separated by freshly painted white plaster, giving the house a reverse Old English-style look—wider planks and a smaller amount of plaster.

As I turned into the driveway, I could hear the gravel crackling under my tires. I turned off my engine and sat, looking straight ahead. The morning rays were glimmering on the water, giving the surface of the lake a shimmering glow that resembled the flames of a fire. I had finally arrived at the one place on this earth where I had ever been able to exhale—a little. *Home.*

As captivating as the scenery was; it was the air and the soft ebb and flow of the lake that instantly sent me into a trance of some sort. The sound of the water fountain trickling back into the lake and the loud crescendo of the birds awakening for the day surrounded me. I removed my shoes and walked through the immaculate grass. The fresh morning dew was cool on my feet; it alleviated the throbbing ache I had failed to recognize earlier. I walked around and touched some of the flowers from the properly tended flowerbeds my mother cared for. As I approached, I reached out to them. The royal blue of the lupine flower reflected its color from the beaded water drops that rested on its petals. The droplets left the tips of my fingers damp. I raised them to my nose and inhaled the sweet, delicate aroma of the flower. I walked around to her beautiful arrangement of peonies and dahlias, which resided closest to the lake. The pinks and reds complemented each other—so beautiful.

For a moment, I stood there and wished I could possess the same ability as her. I instantly killed anything my fingers touched, but she had a gift with plants. She could revive anything, no matter how deteriorated it was. She couldn't fix herself worth a dime, but when people brought her their plants, she would work her magic; she always brought them back to life.

I wound my way down to the dock, my gait slightly faster due to the descending slope of the lawn. My feet made shallow thuds upon the wooden dock, the echo thundering from the water as I walked to the edge. I sat down, allowing my feet to dangle. The crisp water sent a shock through my body, forcing me to take a deep breath. My gaze traveled from the clear, fresh water to the rolling tree hills that surrounded me. The trees cast their reflections upon the water; the sun illuminated the endless arrays of jade, forest, and hunter greens that enveloped the shore, creating a natural contrast with the powder blue of the lake. The water rippled underneath the chaotic movement of the insects.

I sat on the dock peering into the depths of the pristine water, training my eyes to see beyond the obvious. The subtle shadows of perch and sunfish appeared underneath the dock; their skittish nature made them retreat the moment I moved my toes. I smiled at their quirky appearance.

From beyond the treeline, the eerie tremolo call of a common loon could be heard—a pair of them resided in the back cove—and the sound reverberated across the lake. I could imagine them awkwardly making their way to the shoreline, entering the water with grace and ease, leaving the nest out of necessity for the first fish of the morning. The sound washed over me.

The common loon is my favorite bird. I love how they find a mate and remain with it until one of them doesn't return. I love how graceful they are in the water, how capable they are of propelling themselves like torpedoes to catch their prey. Yet, they lack the ability to stand firmly on land. They are very similar to other birds in the duck family but they remain special, for their feet stick out far behind them and their bones are dense. I've always felt a connection to the loon: special, *no*, but I was very different, and only a person looking beyond the surface could tell. Occasionally, someone would see that I was not whole, that my eyes could tell stories, but they would never be capable of knowing what I had inside. *They wouldn't understand.*

The brisk upturn of the wind brought me back. I shivered, wrapped my arms around my body, and made my way back up to the house.

***

The house was silent, but I saw the remnants of the previous night. Bottles of Coors Light were spread across the kitchen counter. From the entrance, I could see other bottles that had been left in front of the fireplace. The stench of cigarette smoke invaded my nostrils. *It must have been a long night*, I thought to myself.

My mother drank a lot. It was usually pleasant to have a couple of drinks with her . . . until she continued drinking. From beers three to five, she remained somewhat pleasant, but very opinionated. After the sixth or seventh beer, she would become ornery. More often than not, she would cause a scene and become verbally—and at times physically—abusive with whomever was there. Sometimes she would abruptly change and become extremely melancholic; it certainly kept everyone on their toes.

I wondered which type of scene had occurred.

I made my way to the living room with the wastebasket. I gathered all the corpses, then grabbed the broom and swept the cigarette ashes and all the soot that had spilled on the floor. I rearranged the couch and prepared the kindling wood in the fireplace. I took a step back—I was pleased. The place looked void of any residual effects of the night before. I hoped, in a way, that I had magically dissipated the events of the previous night.

After the living room cleanup, I disposed of the waste in the kitchen. I contemplated cleaning that too, but I could finally feel my body weakening. The effects of the drugs had completely worn off, and that meant I could sleep. I dragged my body upstairs, where snoring reverberated throughout the corridor. I silently proceeded to shower and put my depleted self to bed.

I awoke with the heat of the beaming sunshine on my face. I must have forgotten to close the blinds. I rubbed my eyes and squinted to see what time it was. I reached around the side of the bed and patted the ground, looking for my phone: quarter after four. My first thought was of her.

"I wonder if she went to work?" I mumbled to myself.

The answer to my question was immediately revealed; I knew she was at work, for the smell of her perfume, Exclamation, lingered. I would have the house to myself for another forty-five minutes if I was lucky. My body still felt weakened from the side effects of the night shift and the drugs, but I rolled out of bed and flopped my feet onto the ground. I dragged myself to the bathroom, finding the task quite demanding. I then made my way to the sink, where I splashed my face with cold water. I peered out the dormer window to the lake as I wiped my face; it was a beautiful, bright day. The stillness of the water disclosed that not a breeze was to be found. At that moment, all was quiet.

I smiled.

She had left her entire makeup kit spread across the vanity, and a slew of discarded clothes on the floor. *She must have been late*, I thought.

I cleaned up her mess, taking care to replace everything in the manner that she would have displayed it. I grabbed my bathrobe from the back of the door and went downstairs. The kitchen was impeccable. I deducted that Malcolm had probably cleaned it up before he left for work. He was a drinker too, but he always went to work on time. He was dependable, mostly responsible, and he loved his job. He was a great man, and one who was slow to anger. Perfect for my instigating, nit-picking mother.

Malcolm was the only man my mother had ever been with who I considered a decent human being. He had never raised a hand to her, nor would he ever.

I recall the first time I ever overheard her on the phone with him. I had just come home from school to find her in her room with the door closed. I had no idea who she was talking to, and her behavior was out of character. I could hear her *giggling*—she didn't giggle. That alone told me she was talking to someone *significant*, and that something was going to happen, for sure.

My mother waited until after my prom to tell me she had met a man and would be moving almost three hours away. I had two choices: either I could move Up North with her and go live with her cousin, or I could ask my aunt if she would take me in. I decided to follow her Up North. We moved two weeks after that conversation. I couldn't live with her and Malcolm for a while until they found a suitable place to rent. He lived with his parents, and it would have been too much for them to take in my mother *and* me.

I was no stranger to coming in second to an array of number ones. I never really had a choice; she had made up her mind and was starting a new life with this man I had not met. I initially protested lightly but quickly retreated; she made her total disregard for my opinion on the matter very clear.

***

I put two spoons of instant coffee into my favorite mug (emblazoned with the phrase *BITE ME*) and poured boiled water over the top. Then, I opened the French doors to the back porch; not even a hint of breeze, as previously noted. The fresh air and sounds of nature flooding into the house felt wonderful. I sat on the steps looking out. The last remnants of summer remained unchanged, apart from the slight shift in the essence of the air. The wind would start coming from the north soon. Sweltering days would give way to tepid ones, then the leaves would turn amber, crimson, and lemon. People would come from around the world to witness the magnificence of Mother Earth's composition. Then, the frigid northern winter would be upon us once again. During that season, there would be a lull for a moment; the north would be quiet and the ski village nearly destitute. Within that lull, residents could enjoy the rare silence . . .

Just then, I heard the hum of a vehicle approaching. I didn't have to peer out toward the lane to know that my mother was almost home; the booming of her county music shattered the silence of the lake. Her energy demanded space. It enveloped everything in its way, swallowing the silence, calm, and ease—chewing it up and spitting it out, making everything in its proximity stagger about for its wits.

She soon appeared on the side of the porch with a cigarette wedged between her lips and her hands full of grocery bags. "Hey sweetie," she called as she dropped a few bags on the ground. She reached up to gently remove the cigarette that was about to ash on her chest. She shifted the ashes methodically toward the ashtray.

"Hey Mom, how's it going?" I said while giving her a hug.

"Mmm, I'm happy you're home, sweetie. I hope I didn't wake you this morning," she said quickly to avoid lingering on the subject. She leaned back and narrowed her eyes at me. "You look pale, what have you been doing to yourself again?"

Her question was more of a rhetorical one. She was well aware of *some* of my indiscretions. We were *mostly* open with each other about our lives, often stating that we were the best of friends—something I whole-heartedly believed.

I looked at her and shrugged. "Nothing really, I worked at the bar last night. It was a long shift and I didn't get out until five a.m." I omitted any mention of the drugs.

"You damned well know I wish you wouldn't work in that sleazy bar. There are plenty of other places you could bartend at if you wanted, and I would feel much better if you would choose *any* other bar." She paused to remove her shoes and light another cigarette. In her eyes, we were superior to *that* kind of bar.

"Mom, I know, I know. You've told me a gazillion times, but I make way more money at the club and I need that cash so I don't have to work like a lunatic all year while I'm finishing my studies. It's my last year, and I just want to have a little cushion." I whined.

"Sweetie, please," she interrupted. "I've basically worked in bars my whole life *and* owned my own bar. I know damn well that you could make nearly as much working somewhere else. I don't like the lowlifes over there. You know Malcolm use to sell coke for them?" She raised her eyebrows and gave me her famous implacable stare. It was the kind of stare that would make a grown man quiver, but I had seen that look a thousand times before. Sometimes it would unsettle me, just a little, but not today.

"Yes, I'm well aware of that fact," I rolled my eyes.

"Don't roll your eyes at me; you're not a kid anymore." She softened her stare. "I'm just saying, I could get you a job at The Gem. Its safer," she cajoled as she winked at me and smiled.

"I appreciate your help, Mom, BUT . . . I don't want to work in a bar. I'm not gonna stay at the strippers much longer; in fact, I think this was my last shift. Plus, I can handle myself—c'mon," I winked. "Anyway, I really just wanted to wrap up the summer with a little extra cash so I'm not plowing through my loans. I already told you this," I said, exasperated.

She came and sat with me on the steps. She wrapped her arm around my shoulders and leaned in for a side hug. "I'm just so happy you're home."

"Me too." I reciprocated the hug.

I enjoyed the ease I found within these docile moments, when she stopped criticizing everything. During these times, she and I found comfort and surrender within the safety of our bubble; transparent, each aware and accepting of the other's foibles. We lingered there, both of us momentarily silent.

"Well, I'll help you get this stuff in—did you get anything for me?" I grinned.

"Of course. I'm going to prepare some of your favorite meals this week, so you'll have plenty of food you can bring back with you," she smiled. This was her way of nurturing me; cooking had always been her way of saying *I love you.*

"I appreciate it, Mom. I'll help."

***

We each grabbed several bags. Then, packed like mules, we trekked them across the dinning room into the kitchen. Resting against the pantry were three twenty-four-pack cases of beer. The sight made me grimace as I tried to avoid the phantom blow that caused my stomach to churn. She noticed my scowl and followed my line of sight.

"They had a sale," she said nonchalantly. She turned her back to avoid my eyes; the change in the air was palpable.

I chose to ignore the falsehood of her statement. I had become quite the expert at diverting uncomfortable situations, and full-out avoided the topic of alcohol with her.

She was an alcoholic—a *functioning alcoholic*, to be precise. That simply meant that, by definition, she maintained a job, a home, and somewhat of a family life. She could go through the daytime without a drop of alcohol. During the times she had to be a productive member of society, she seemed totally normal from an outsider's perspective; slightly on edge, but "normal."

Typically, after seven p.m., she would be drunk. From the time she got home from work until she could barely stand, she binge-drank. She drank *every* night.

Fun fact: Approximately one in thirteen adults suffers from alcohol abuse, and about seven million children live in a household with at least one adult who has an alcohol use disorder. Lovely, isn't it?

I redirected the conversation to more neutral grounds; avoidance and ignorance were key to a successful relationship with my mother.

"So, what's first?

Mac 'n cheese is a must. I really want a few jars of spaghetti sauce, too," I cajoled.

She flashed a relieved smile and the mood in the kitchen returned to a pleasant state.

"Sounds good. You grab those veggies over there, and I'll get the pots."

She flowed gracefully through the kitchen from one task to the next, effortlessly completing each task at hand with such beautiful serenity displayed on her face; she was in her element. Rarely did I get to enjoy a sight quite like this. We spent the remainder of the evening preparing food together. The pleasant atmosphere was invigorating, and I really enjoyed her company and our conversations. She was wise and full of cynicism about the world, but she always tried to encourage me to succeed. She showered me with love and acceptance. Gosh, I felt so lucky to have such an amazing bond with her.

Malcolm arrived a few hours into our crusade. The muted screeching of the door alerted my mother to his presence. Her pupils instantly dilated. Her energy shifted. Her entire pleasant demeanor gave way to the ferocious stance of a cornered puma. She reached into the fridge and grabbed her first beer of the night; it was quite impressive that she had held on this long without opening one. I wondered if her self-restraint from touching the bottle for so long felt anything to her like the resounding anxiety which flooded my existence felt to me.

"It smells delicious in here," Malcolm exclaimed as he entered the kitchen and put his hand on my shoulder. “Hey Soph,” he squeezed me lightly. “How did you sleep?” His chocolate-walnut eyes peered into mine, genuinely caring.

“I don’t really think I can count that as sleeping. I think it’s more like I passed out. But hey, that counts too, right?”

He tapped my shoulder like a consoling coach.

My mother’s back was turned to us. She fiddled with some jars in the corner, trying with all her might to avoid him.

“Hey babe,” he said gently, testing her as he walked over and kissed her on the side of her temple. Her body tensed. I, in turn, shifted from foot to foot, wondering if I should exit the kitchen and retreat somewhere safe, or if she would be civil. No one—and I mean *no one*—really knew why she was so angry at him all the time. I hypothesized that it was because he was a safe place for her to regurgitate all her pent-up resentment, anger, and hurt toward men.

Paul would be proud of my insight.

She stood immobile as his hand remained on her waist. The events of the previous night didn’t matter to him. He forgave and forgot, leaving no room for pestilent matters to linger. It was an act I highly envied, and one which I assume repulsed my mother. He leaned in and whispered something in her ear. I didn’t quite make out what it was, but she turned and tilted her face so she was staring directly into his eyes. Her eyebrows raised, and she just stared. He was unwavering; he simply smiled at her and brought her body as close to his as possible.

“I love you, woman. Now just breathe.” He kissed her and just like that, her body surrendered and she softened—*a little.*

That was exactly why Malcolm was amazing. *Right there.*

"Well, I'm going to jump in the shower. I have to DJ tonight at the bar. Sophie, are you joining?" he asked while still embracing her.

"Umm, I don't know yet. I think I may stay in tonight and just hang out."

My mother interjected. "Nonsense, I know you two and I damned well know that you want to go, Sophie Ann," she scolded.

Malcolm and I looked at each other, grinning as she kindly chastised us.

"Mom, why don't you come too? It could be fun, and I'll play you some country music." I waited expectantly.

"Not tonight, sweetie. I'll stay in, but you can go."

I looked at Malcolm.

"Well, you women do whatever you like, I have to go shower now. I still smell like bait." He sniffed his hands and laughed, making me laugh and annoying her.

I really wanted to go, but at the same time, I knew I would be staying home unless she was coming. She fared better if someone was watching her. Although she seemed in pretty good spirits that night, I knew her better than that.

"It's all good, Mom, I'd much rather spend time with you." I winked and gave her a cuddle.

"Ya, right!" she retorted as she rolled her eyes.

"Oh my god, did you just roll your eyes at me? You didn't!" I over-exaggerated my facial expression of disbelief, making her laugh. She reached into the fridge and grabbed herself two beers.

"You have one for me there, or is that all for you?" I pointed at her bottles.

"You are more then welcome to take your own."

I did.

She sat herself comfortably in her usual spot in front the fireplace. We had placed the loveseat facing it, just for her. She loved the smell of the fire and the crackling sounds it made. Also, it was the only place in the house where we could smoke. Malcolm didn't smoke, and he detested the smell, but he had given up trying to make her do anything that she didn't want to do. He had tried for a long time to make her go outside, but she couldn't be bothered. He was tired of fighting and he knew she wouldn't cede, so he did.

I stroked the match and lit the kindling wood. Soon, the candescent glow beamed on our faces. Within ten seconds, she lit two smokes and handed me one.

Malcolm came downstairs, and with him the discernible odor of his Drakkar Noir cologne. He stood behind us, unbuttoned the cuffs of his sleeves, and rolled them partway up, displaying his muscular forearms.

"Well girls, who's coming with?" He tucked his shirt into his buffalo jeans.

"Looking good—not bad for an old man," I teased. He was neither old nor bad-looking. He was, in fact, ten years my mother's junior.

"Ah, thanks," he smirked.

My mother got up without saying a word. She retrieved two more bottles from the refrigerator then sat back down, lighting another cigarette with the butt of her other smoke, which wasn't even finished yet.

"So, babe, I take it you're not coming then?"

She replied *no* without looking at him. We both ignored her.

"How about you, Soph? Wanna come play some music tonight?"

I shook my head. "Nah, not tonight, sorry." I was disappointed. The twenty-one-year-old girl wanted to go out and have some fun, maybe bust a move or two. But as my mother's daughter, I was bound to protect her—from herself. It was an obligation that was bestowed upon me from within the womb; etched within me, branding me for life.

I looked at Malcolm and shrugged my shoulders. He smiled sympathetically, kissed my mother on the head, and left for the bar.

***

My mother and I sat in silence, watching *Reba* reruns. I was still sipping on my first beer. Mother, on the other hand, was on her fifth, or maybe her sixth. I'm not sure, but I knew she was feeling it a little by then.

"Mom, are you okay?" I asked.

She turned to face me, "Of course, I'm okay. Why?"

Her eyes were glossy as she stared at me. Her elbow rested on her knee, the cigarette dangling between her fingers swayed slightly.

"Because you seem upset today. I'm worried about you. Why don't you talk to someone?" I quietly suggested.

Her eyes squinted. "Talk to someone about *what*? I have nothing to say and there's nothing wrong," she snapped.

God, she was so persistently aggravating. I had tried countless times to convince her to speak with a therapist. I even went ahead and scheduled appointments for her, only to have her not show up. After a handful of attempts, I gave up.

I exhaled mildly loudly, slightly annoyed. "Okay then."

The crackling of the fire filled the silence. After a while, and beer number eight, she turned to me and began to lecture.

"I don't like you working at that bar. I don't want you to let those *nasty* men use you. You're better than me; I don't want you repeating the same things I did." She took a sip. "I'm telling you, Soph, nobody, and I mean *nobody*, gives a fuck about you in this world like I do. My girl, you gotta finish that degree of yours and get yourself a good life. Look at me: I'm nothing. I'm pure *crap*. The only good thing I ever did right in this world was having you and your brother. Your brother won't even talk to me, you know." Streams of tears flowed down her cheeks.

I sat quietly, intently listening to her.

"It breaks my heart. Every day it breaks my heart, Sophie." Her voice was pitchy and trembling. "And I can't do anything to fix it, you know. I just can't undo the hurt that I've caused that boy . . . the hurt that I've put you kids through. None of it. None of it . . ."

There it was, finally showing itself from the veil of the shadows—the real torment.

I scooted closer to her and wrapped my arms around her shoulders. For a moment, she leaned into me and sniffled. I sat there silently embracing her, weathering the impending storm that was inflicting so much pain. I silently shed tears of my own. This wasn't about me, or about the actual damage that had been done to my brother and myself. *This was about her* and her inability to forgive herself for reprehensible choices she had made that had caused us to suffer. This was her habitual self-inflicted onslaught. I just stood fast and held her until she could come to grips with reality. Her outburst lasted only a few moments, but those minutes seemed to stretch for an eternity.

She raised her dampened face, and muttered *I'm so sorry, sweetie.* I took the bottle from her hands and set it on the floor. I placed her arm over my shoulders and held her up.

"Come on, Mom. Let's get you to bed, okay?"

She complied, weakened from the emotions and the booze. I placed her in her bed, fully clothed, and tucked her in. I bent over and gave her three kisses, a ritual I had performed my entire life: a kiss on the left cheek, a kiss on the forehead, and another on the right cheek. She gave me a faint smile and turned to her side. Almost instantly, she was asleep.

I stood in the darkness of her bedroom, gathering my thoughts and picking myself up. I had been through these enactments *many, many* times. They never ceased to be difficult. I wished and prayed; for her, and for myself. I wanted her to find peace. Maybe if she found a way to forgive herself, I could in turn begin to heal. I didn't know what to do. I was a little girl trapped in a woman's body. I was mortified of the world around me, but I held so many responsibilities.

They were heavy.

I felt heavy.

My mind flashed back to a moment in time so long ago, I shouldn't even have been capable of remembering it, but I did . . .

"I want to see my mommy," my minuscule voice demanded. We were parked in the visitors parking lot of a hospital. I was only three years old. My aunt turned to me, and in her sweetest voice she said, "No sweetie, not today, okay?" It wasn't okay, but I had no choice in the matter. She got out of the van and I watched her disappear into the building. My little self sat in the seat of the van and cried for my mother. The constriction in my chest made me feel like I would spontaneously implode. I thought I would never see my mommy again.

She had been pushed in front of a van. She had something like three fractures to her pelvis, a broken wrist, some cracked ribs, and a bruised-up face. The doctors had called her *lucky* . . .

I snapped back to reality, shook my head, and went to my room, where I got dressed. *Fuck this shit, I'm going out.*

***

The bar was vibrating with music. Malcolm was one of the best DJs in town. He had tons of charisma and he loved music. His face lit up with a giant smile as he saw me enter the bar.

"Sophie, you changed your mind!" He gave me a hug.

"Ya, Mom's sleeping, so I figured I'd come out for some fun with my favorite dad." He liked that I referred to him as my dad. He was amazing, and he taught me so much.

He didn't need me to elaborate on the events of the night, or why I had left the house. It was a common theme we shared. Instead, he chose to take my mind off things.

"Here, you fade in the next track." He stepped aside so I could approach the control panel. I faded the song into Ram Jam's "Black Betty," one of my personal favorite songs, and typically my go-to when rockin' the old-school stuff. A few people in the crowd shouted *Yay!* Malcolm lit up the mic:

"Give it up for my daughterrrr! I'm *DJ Malcolm*, here for your entertainment. If you have any special requests, we'll be here until closing." He muted the mic and smiled.

The whirlwind of the night and the thrill of being Malcolm's assistant DJ alleviated some of the weight I carried. Malcolm could relate to the burden of loving my mother. I was grateful for the respite. We closed the bar in the early morning and headed home.

***

The lake was pristine and the sun glistened brightly, making the surface of the water shimmer. It was a perfect day to be out on the lake to try our luck at catching some fish, although we all knew that we didn't need luck, as Malcolm was manning the ship. He was an avid outdoorsman, and in my opinion, a fish whisperer. He could catch a fish in the middle of a drought, I kid you not.

Mother and I lazily rested our legs over the side of the boat, each of us holding a fishing rod in one hand and a beer in the other. She looked as though she were about to perform a daring juggling act. From time to time, I watched her from beneath my sunglasses. All three of us sat in complete silence; all that could be heard was the faint humming of the electric motor. The boat slowly swayed with the soft rippling of the water. A swift jerk of the rod interrupted the silence; Malcolm had hooked a fish.

"I got one. Oh, he's a big one!" His foot rested on the edge of the boat, his excitement permeated around us. He reeled the fish all the way to the side of the boat. "Soph, grab that net, come on now, he's not gonna hold for long. He's barely hooked. Ah, *little son of a gun*, you're not going anywhere!" With each passing second, his voice intensified.

I reached over the edge and scooped the fish. "Oh my god, it's a monster!" I shrieked.

My mother sat up and exclaimed, "Way to go, babe! Holy shit. That *is* a monster!"

The silver and gold scales of the three-foot pike glittered as we pulled it into the boat.

"Now we can have a feast for your last night home. What a catch!" Malcolm was as giddy as a kid.

Everyone was happy.

That afternoon was spent enjoying the sunshine and each other's company. The conversations flowed easily without any lurking issues. These moments were few and far between. Malcolm and Mom were attempting to display their best behavior, more than likely because they didn't want to ruin my last night at home. At least I liked to believe that I was important enough that they would consider my well-being. *Maybe.*

"So, Soph—are you happy to be getting back to school?" Malcolm asked while preparing the pike for our fish fry.

"Ya, I guess. I just hope I'll make it to end of this year. It's tedious." I leaned against the kitchen counter in between the two of them.

"You're a smart girl, you'll do just fine. Just stay away from all those college parties, and the other *you-know-what*, and you should make it out in one piece." Malcolm giggled at his own remarks.

"HA. HA. Very funny. I don't participate in *those* activities nearly as much as you guys assume I do. So shhh." *It was a lie.*

He turned his gaze toward me. I smiled and winked at him.

"Sophie, we all know what you're up to when you're away. You're a grown woman, and I hope to hell that I raised you well enough to make better decisions for yourself." Mom had to put her two cents in.

"Of course, Mother. You raised me oh-SO-well, I'm nearly perfection!" I said sarcastically. She swatted me on the wrist.

She and Malcolm worked simultaneously, preparing supper.

"Can I do anything to help?" I asked whoever was listening.

"Ya, you can grab me a beer out of the fridge please, sweetie," Mother gestured with her head.

"Make that two," Malcolm added.

I complied with their requests. Allowing myself to be as flawed as they were, I grabbed a beer for myself, too. I pondered whether we were all just trying to find our way out of the internal abyss that swallowed us; all just trying to find respite within the never-ceasing labyrinth of self destruction and chaos. Sometimes, one of us would cast a buoy out to another before total annihilation occurred, only to be propelled into their own incessant nightmare. We loved each other—there was no question about it—but the damage we caused to others around us was baffling. We were enablers of self-sabotage and low self-esteem, incapable of stopping the inevitable collisions of our own existences. Mother and I were the rats that spread the plague, and our subconscious minds tried to eradicate us by igniting the poor choices we made, but we just couldn't be that easily destroyed. We had superhuman powers, and a shitload of moxie.

CHAPTER 3

"Oh my god, I can't believe this is our last year. I totally can NOT wait until its over, and the first week isn't even done yet." Chelsea gave the best re-enactment of sheer misery she possible could before she flung her purse and books onto the desk beside me.

"Come on now, we got this. Plus, we can't fuckin' quit now, dude; it would literally be like watching the last three years of ours lives burn up in flames and laughing about it. It would be slightly psychotic." We both laughed, then I got up and gave her a hug.

Chelsea and I had hit it off instantly during the first week of school three years prior. On the first day of classes, I saw her making out with her boyfriend against the lockers. I was a girl that came from instability and low self-esteem, and here she was—so at ease with herself. The hustle and bustle happening around the happy couple was of no interest to either of them.

I was immediately envious of her calm demeanor and her confidence; I wanted to know how to be like that. We took a liking to each other and since then had been awesome college buddies. I couldn't fathom what my college experience would have been like if it hadn't been for her. Albeit, we didn't always do the most responsible things, and there was always one of us initiating some kind of tomfoolery, but there was a comfort in knowing that we had each other's backs, regardless of the mess we were in.

Like the time Chels called me up, asking me to come pick her up at some random guy's house because she couldn't recall how she got there and didn't know where her car was. I flew down the highway doing over a hundred and forty clicks to come to her rescue. It was a pure, no-judgement, elbows-deep, no-bullshit kind of friendship.

I would do anything for that girl.

"So, how was your summer?" she asked as she leaned in and rested her head in her hand.

"Ah, you know. It was all right. I worked a ton and I partied a little. And, you know, had some fun," I giggled.

Chelsea pushed me on the shoulder. "You had *some fun*? What kind of *fun* are you talking about? I thought you and Elijah were gonna try the whole long-distance thing? I'm totally out of the loop then, what the hell?"

I shrugged. "Nah, I didn't want to bother with the whole long-distance thing. It doesn't work. I really didn't want to be tied down, on top of working and shit. No way."

What you really mean to say is: you bailed out . . .

At that moment, I thought about Solange. I wondered if she was okay—I hoped that she was. I also thought about Vicky, Julien, and what's-his-name . . . anyway . . .

Chelsea looked at me quizzically. "Well, we have a whole bunch of time to discuss this new-found freedom of yours," she winked. Then, in a muffled tone, "But for now, don't look. You-know-*who*'s coming toward you." She cleared her throat and turned to aimlessly look through her purse, as though she were so lost in the task at hand that she couldn't be bothered to look at who was standing four feet from us.

Elijah approached our desks, followed by the girls Chels and I called the Groupies, because for some reason, this man had the gifts of a snake charmer and everyone loved him. He really didn't have Hollywood looks, but his chiseled jaw, dirty brown hair and steel-blue eyes complimented his charismatic and attentive personality—something that women tend to adore. So, it was easy to see why he was most certainly likable. I, in turn, had also fallen for him. I had wanted to find someone who would save me from myself. *Someone to replace my ex*. It seemed that he liked my I-don't-give-a-fuck attitude. He found it amusing— challenging. My smart-ass comments that no man could ever tame me made me even more appealing.

Elijah had taken it upon himself to prove me wrong about men. He would be *the man* who would change my outlook on the male species . . . or so he thought. We had been an item for some time before summer break. The fact that he had "conquered" me led to his self-entitlement and arrogance, not to mention an oh-so-inflated ego. All of that combined caused way too many disputes and full-out vicious verbal fights. He didn't like to be dismissed, and I didn't like anyone trying to control me. I felt suffocated when someone tried to love me, and he deeply wanted to love me. Or was it something else?

We were very flawed individuals, and like water and oil, we didn't mix. But for some reason, we kept trying. The whole dysfunction and intensity of our passionate affair must have had something to do with the fact that we kept coming back. We were mutually addicted to the adrenaline rush that our tremulous relationship offered. They say you continue to attract what you think you deserve, and you do what you know best. It's the whole 'vicious cycle' thing. I agreed with that train of thought; it was the most definite, accurate representation of the choices I made and the people I dated. Happiness and ease were foreign concepts to me. I had come to understand that I was so very flawed that I couldn't so much as touch *those ideals*.

"I see you're alive, obviously since you're sitting right there." He towered over me, intently waiting for my reaction.

"I sure am," I said with a sly grin.

"Why the hell didn't you call back this summer? I just don't get it. Why do you do this?" He stood there awaiting some sort of revelation. I had none to give, really. All I wanted was for class to begin so this uncomfortable interaction could be put off indefinitely.

"I already told you why. We don't need to be hanging our dirty laundry for the entire class to hear. Its all good—we all know I'm the horrible person that did you wrong, there are plenty of witnesses, and I'm sure that you let everyone know. Now can we be done with this scene?" I stared at him in defiance.

It seemed that everyone had chosen sides before classes resumed; I just hadn't received the memo that I needed to rally for some supporters. Not that I would have done any rallying at all, because let's be honest, I couldn't give two shits about who wanted to be on my side. I couldn't stand all this idle gossip and the trifling, so-called friendships. He could have the entire classroom for all I cared.

I had Chelsea and Kyle—I was set.

"Fine, be that way," he huffed as he turned to take his seat.

"God, that was unbearable," I said to Chelsea through gritted teeth.

"Don't sweat it, hun. He'll be all over you before the end of the month."

Meh, she probably had a point. That's usually what happened. I was hoping that this time, I could just be done with it and not cave in . . . but I didn't know how to be alone. Then again, I didn't know how to be with another person, either. If it wasn't going to be Elijah, it would be someone else . . .

"Okay everyone, welcome back. I hope you guys had a great time relaxing this summer. There will be no time for bullshit this semester; you guys have your work cut out. No slacking," the professor immediately began his dictum as he entered the classroom. Chelsea and I looked at each other with raised eyebrows.

"*Holy shit*," came a mutual mutter.

***

"So, pre-drinking at my place, then?" I asked.

I held my cell phone between my shoulder and my ear as I looked through my closet. "I have absolutely nothing to wear, Chels."

Not even a full seven days in and we had already jumped right back on the bandwagon where we had left off. A whole lot of partying and a limited amount of sleep—which meant a whole lot of drugs to compensate.

She sighed. "You always say that, but you always look hot."

There was no compliment in this entire world that could have made me feel comfortable in my own skin. "Please, don't humor me. Arrggg, I wanna go, but I don't wanna go. You know?" I paused; I could hear her irritation.

Chelsea was incapable of understanding the sentiment of feeling absolutely disgusted with oneself. She was the embodiment of self confidence: money, beauty, brains, and a great family. This girl was everything I wished I could be.

"Come on Soph, I'll bring over some of my things and you can have an array of choices. There's no way in hell we are gonna miss the first Thursday and then miss out on all the fun tonight." She paused, her voice filled with excitement and expectation.

"You're right, it will be great once we start drinking, and I'll ease up, I promise." I agreed, reluctantly.

"Yay, I can't wait! I'll be over in forty-five minutes. Love you babe." She hung up the phone without hearing my reply.

In the silence of my bachelor apartment, I stood in front of the full-length mirror. I tried to gaze at my own reflection for a mere moment, trying to see the so-called hottie Chelsea had mentioned. I forced myself to look carefully before it became unbearable. A repugnant wave invaded my body with such intensity I was on the verge of throwing up. Just then, the phone rang. I picked it up without looking at the caller I.D.

Chels must have forgotten something.

"Hey," I said.

The blaring of county music shot through the speakers.

"Sweetie, whatcha doing?" she slurred slightly, her voice deepened by the effects of the booze. I peered at my clock: nine p.m. Of course she would be drunk by now.

"Hey, Mom. Nothing much; I'm just getting ready to go out. How are you?" I took a seat.

"Oh, I'm good, you know. I just wanted to know how the return to classes was going." I could hear the flicker of her lighter. "It's just so lonely without you here. Soph." she complained.

I could feel her anxiety lingering below the surface. She was having a down in-the-dumps kind of night. "I know, Mom."

The responsibility I had toward her was never-ceasing, despite the distance that separated us. She was incapable of functioning through her own thoughts the moment she picked up the bottle. I was her lighthouse—her navigational aid through her obsidian nights. Yet, my foundation was weak, and I wouldn't stand fast forever.

As the years passed and these types of exchanges between us danced on and on, I could feel myself dwindling a little more with each intervention, and with my every effort of damage control, she seemed to worsen, too.

I sat on my futon with my hands on my forehead, "Where's Malcolm, Mom?" I asked, trying to find a solution.

She made a retching sound. I could envision her acting out the movement of putting her finger in her mouth to produce the fake action of vomiting.

"He went to bed." Her voice became vile. "Anyway, I'll let you have fun, be safe out there," she said curtly.

I exhaled strenuously. "Okay, Mom. Why don't you get some sleep? Get some rest and you'll feel better tomorrow. I'll call you after classes, okay?" I felt uneasy but tried to reassure her that she wasn't alone. I was there for her.

"Ya, I'll get some sleep now, I love you, sorry sweetie." The shame transpired through her apologies.

"It's okay, Mom. Love you too, Mom." The silence was heavy. I rested my head in my hands. Exhaustion crept through my body. I shut my eyes tightly, trying to prevent the memory from overtaking my thoughts…

***

"Promise me you're gonna call if you need a ride home, okay? I'll keep the phone close by," my sixteen-year old self chastised her.

She stared at me scornfully. "Sometimes I wonder if you realize that I am YOUR mother, not the other way around, young lady." She placed her hands on her hips. "I will be home late tonight, and I'm NOT going to call you—you have to get up for work. So, don't worry."

"Please, Mom. At least don't drive home if you've had too much, okay?" I pleaded.

Her stare softened. "Of course, sweetheart. I promise."

I remained dubious. "Have a great night, Mom. You deserve it. Happy fortieth birthday."

She hugged me and walked out.

I awoke in the early morning to the stillness of our apartment. There was no sign of her, so I checked her room. Her bed was neatly made. I checked the answering machine; she hadn't left any messages. I could feel the panic rising within my chest. The ache seized my entire being, and for a moment I was paralyzed. After a few seconds, I let out a short scream.

"FUCK." I looked at the time; it was six-fifteen. I had to get ready for work.

***

At nine-thirty a.m. I called home. No answer.

At eleven a.m. I called home again. No answer. I decided to call my aunt to see if she had heard anything. I was just barely keeping my composure. The phone rang and rang, then finally, someone picked up. My uncle's voice boomed through the receiver. "Hello?"

"Uncle, it's me. Umm, I'm just wondering if Auntie is around?" I asked anxiously.

He cleared his throat. "Hey, Sophie. Umm, listen, your aunt is gonna come see you later, okay?"

My heart was pounding. My ears were buzzing.

"Okay, I just want to know if anyone's seen Mom? I left for work this morning and she still hadn't come home, and I called twice already—"

He cut me off before I could continue. "Soph, your mom is fine. Your aunt will come and see you at work, okay?"

I had so many questions I wanted answers for, but I could tell he didn't want to get into anything further. So, I reluctantly complied. "Okay, Uncle. Thanks."

***

It was a little after one p.m. when my aunt showed up at my work. I could tell immediately that something had happened. I had seen her contorted, pain-stricken face many times before. I wasn't the only casualty that my mother left behind during her bouts of self-absorbed destructive behaviors. I stood silently, waiting.

She dove right in.

"Soph, sweetie, your mother drove her car into a ditch this morning." She paused, but I knew she wouldn't spare me. I had lived with this chaos my entire life. I knew how to take a blow. I braced for impact.

"She was drunk. She flipped her car. The ambulance brought her to the hospital. They said she was lucky she came out nearly unscathed."

There was that word again: *lucky*.

"The booze made her so limp she just bounced around. They said that if she were sober, it could have been fatal." My aunt took a deep breath and exhaled it loudly, as though her chest could not bear the weight. Then, she continued.

"She was released from the hospital and charged with a DUI. I bailed her out. She got her licence revoked. I brought her home, and now she's resting." My aunt stared at her feet; I could see her gathering her composure.

"I'm sorry, Soph. I'll come over and help out, okay?" she offered quietly, as though she were attempting to coax a child away from a tantrum.

I silently nodded.

The tears flowed down my cheeks. The anger rushed through my veins as I tried to recede the violent outburst waiting to erupt. My aunt walked toward me and wrapped her arms tightly around my body. The lament came from the deepest part of my fragmented being. It raised to the summit of my throat, erupting with fierceness, like the mournful scream of a banshee. It lasted for only a brief moment until I gathered myself.

I inhaled deeply and looked into my aunt's saddened eyes. They resonated a deep sorrow that only someone who loved my mother as much as I did could feel.

"Ya, okay." I cleared my throat and sniffled a few times. "I'm gonna wrap up here and call one of the guys to relieve me. I'll see you later." As I had many times before, I pushed aside my emotions and placed them in the 'don't have time to feel' box.

***

I leaned against my mother's door frame and watched her while she slept. Her broken arm was wrapped in a white cast; it rested over her stomach.

Her eyes were blackened, and from where I stood, I could see a few Steri-Strips on her forehead. I didn't dare wake her. I didn't want to talk to her, anyway. My anger was still all-too-palpable, and the taste of betrayal lingered. So, I went to my room. On my pillow was a note:

Sweetie, I'm so sorry I almost left you alone.
I promise I will never act like that again.
You are so important to me.
My girl, can you ever forgive me?
I love you. Love Mom xxx

***

Chelsea barged into my apartment. "Girl, I cannot wait . . ." her voice trailed off.

My head shot up as her arrival snapped me out of my daze. I must have been holding my breath, because I gasped.

"What the fuck, Soph? Are you okay?" she questioned.

She came and sat beside me, leaning her body into mine. Her expression, concerned.

"I'm gonna be fine. Sorry . . . I . . . I just had a moment," I said, gathering myself.

She waited quietly.

Finally, I slapped her knee. "Okay, so what did you bring me?" I abruptly got up and resumed a pleasant façade.

She squinted at me. "Soph, if you need to talk, it's okay. I'm here," she said softly.

I turned my back to her and walked toward my bistro table to grab my smokes. I lit one and inhaled deeply. I welcomed the instantaneous relief it offered. I stood in my cloud of smoke in silence, trying to get the last reminiscence of my recollection to fuck off. Chelsea went to the kitchen and got us two shots of Jägermeister. She came and sat in the chair in front of me, analyzing the situation. I could sense her gauging her approach, but I let her be. I was too busy trying to gather my thoughts.

"So, you wanna check out what I brought?"

She had opted to sidestep the situation; I appreciated that.

"Oh, I brought that nice, red, lace top you love. Its gonna cheer you up, I'm sure." she played along.

I looked at her, finally capable of offering an exchange. "Sweet. Then I really don't need to look at anything else. I'm set. I love that shirt." I smiled at her, and with that, she seemed to soften up.

"I'm sorry I get weird like this," I said, ashamed.

"What are you talking about? You're always weird, so no worries, babe," she winked.

Once satisfied with my transformation from college casual to ready-to-dance, I reached into my purse and retrieved one of my baggies. I took out one pill of X and swallowed it down. I offered the other to Chels, but she shook her head *no*.

***

The line-up at the club was almost half a block long. Chelsea and I walked past all the people that had been waiting for god-knows-how-long. Some muttered that extreme injustice was occurring, others shouted louder—all of it fell on deaf ears. We walked up to the bouncer at the door and gave him two kisses each.

"Hey, Sam. How are you doing, you sexy stud?" Chels grazed her hand across his chest, flirting.

"I'm doing much better now that I get to see you girls tonight," he winked.

I hung back and giggled. Chelsea was irresistible to men; the reincarnation of Aphrodite's sensuality, seduction, and pleasure. I watched her wrap up her show. She slowly slid her hand down his chest, leaned into him, and gave him a lingered kiss on the cheek.

"Thanks so much, Sam," she said as he side-stepped to let us through.

We wriggled our way through the crowd, saying *hey* to a few people between us and the bar. The music was booming with a mixture of clubbing hip-hop tracks—Akon played as I made my way through the crowd. I rested my body against the bar and leaned over to shout at the barmaid on the other side.

"Hey chick, send two gin and tonics down here please, and three shots of tequila."

She waved in acknowledgement.

My mind and body were beginning to feel the effects of the pill. Chelsea looked at me and laughed out loud. "Girl, you are feeling *good*."

I winked at her as she slammed her three tequila shots back.

"Let's head to the dance floor, I wanna dance!" I grabbed our drinks and motioned for us to get closer. I wanted to snatch up some bar space near the dance floor before it was all taken up.

Plenty of people were already dancing, bumping, and grinding. Everyone mingled and groped whoever was nearest to them—it was a real free-for-all. I made myself a path in between all the bodies colliding with one another and commanded my space. Chels and I locked hands and began dancing. The air in the bar was moist from the excessive amount of people contained in one small space. Some bodies brushed against mine, leaving their clammy sweat behind. Even with the heat radiating through me, the small patches of wetness created chills within my body. I squeezed my eyes shut, welcoming the amplifying high, and swayed with the rhythm of the music, raising my hands up to graze underneath my hairline, allowing the current to cool me. I let the movements flow freely through my body, sensing a lightness that I was incapable of attaining sober. I let myself feel the sensations that encircled me*; I was free.*

Her tap on my shoulder jolted my eyes open. She gave a nudge for me to look to the other side of the bar. “He’s watching you,” Chelsea informed me.

Resting against the wall was Elijah. He stared at me. He didn’t budge when he noticed me looking right back. He took a drink of his beer, contemplating me.

“I really don’t care, Chels. Its not a big deal,” I shouted above the music.

I continued to dance as though I were unaffected by his presence, but I made an effort to seek out a random guy in the crowd.

I found a willing partner and began grinding with him. I wanted to be spiteful and spark some jealousy in Elijah. I looked out from the corner of my eye to see if he was still watching me. He was gone. I turned my focus to the guy in front of me, dismissing the impending encounter. Suddenly, apparently bored with me, the guy stepped back and turned to dance with the girl that was beside him—Chelsea.

I shrugged it off and made my way to where I had left our stuff. As I reached to take a drink, I felt a hand wrap around my waist and move me backward. I turned slightly. My eyes met Elijah's. He pulled me into him, caressed my cheek with the back of his hand, and began swaying us to the rhythm of the song. Placing his hands heavily on my hips, he maneuvered me to his desire. I allowed him to take possession of my body. My senses heightened, my guards lowered, and our surroundings faded into a blurry haze as I could barely contain my arousal. His breath trickled down my neck, inciting my body to yearn for him with feverish intensity. He could sense the electrifying desire surfacing. He slipped his fingers through my hair and kissed me with fervor and appetite.

"I'm taking you home, Soph. *Right now.*" He stared into my eyes, poised with intent.

I nodded, succumbing to temptation with little persuasion

CHAPTER 4

I acquiesced without intending to. Elijah and I restarted our relationship after that night at the bar. Within the week, he had imposed himself back into my apartment—not that I had tried to stop him. I sabotaged the solitude and quiet refuge I had created within my tiny bachelor pad. It had been *my* nook of peace and quiet. I cherished it deeply, *but not enough to say no*. Now, everything was in disarray. The resentment was already escalating. I was angry with myself for being a weakling; for allowing myself to cave for a man who depleted my already non-existent reserves of vitality.

I lay on my futon with the blankets pulled up to my chin, engrossed by the smoke that escaped his nostrils and his mouth as he shouted at the TV. The Montreal Canadians were playing against the Bruins. He sat on the edge of the futon in his boxers, consumed by the game.

"Oh, baby! Did you see that shot?" he shouted at me in excitement.

"That was pretty sweet," I retorted.

I could care less about hockey, but from what I had told Elijah, I was a huge fan. Once upon a time, I had convinced myself that I loved the game. I wanted to please others, and it was always at my own expense.

My likes and dislikes were constantly changing depending on who I was dating, or which crowd I hung out with. I went from an avid tomboy to a punk gothic to a cowgirl to a hip-hop lover to a lesbian . . . all within a two-year span. I couldn't even sit here and tell you what I liked or didn't like.

I didn't have the slightest idea.

Elijah tapped my calf and shook it in excitement. I pulled my leg away from him, turned around, and placed the blankets over my face. Why had I placed the anchor in my hands and thrown myself overboard with it? Barely a few months had passed since our reconciliation and we were already instigating one another—always trying to test the other's patience and tolerance of bullshit. I truthfully couldn't stand the man. He wasn't a bad man per se, we just knew how to attack each other on the rawest levels. We fueled the darkest corners of the other's existence and demanded they show up for the fight. Separate from me, he was a great human: kind, considerate, hardworking, and always willing to help someone out. On the other hand, I just needed to see how far I could test his limits. I manipulated him to see if he would crack. I taunted the demons that lurked beneath. I wanted to know how far could I retaliate against another person's entire being before he would snap—and what would happen if he did? Would he raise his hands to me like I had known men to do? I pushed to know if I could trust. I tested men's boundaries to see what they were made of. I had never trusted one before, and unfortunately, Elijah was no exception. *How much longer would I last in a relationship that I knew was doomed to fail?* I thought to myself

I threw the blankets over my head, hoping that sleep would quickly envelope me.

***

"I don't see you anymore, Soph." Chelsea scowled at me.

I could barely look her in the eyes anymore. With Elijah living with me, I had no more social life. I had limited my contact with my only two friends, I had barely been back home to visit my mother, and I had cancelled my last three appointments with Paul. I was being a shithead and everyone I knew was being let down by some expectation that I wasn't meeting. I didn't have the energy to put up the front for all these different people, so I opted to stay a recluse.

"I know, I'm sorry. It's just uncomfortable when you are in the same place as him. He knows you detest him, and its reciprocal, trust me. So, what do you want me to do?" I looked at her sullenly. "He drives me crazy and honestly, I don't know what the fuck I was thinking. Well, I know what I was thinking that night, but I didn't think that one night would have led me to the slaughterhouse. I just want him to go. I just can't be in a relationship, its too much responsibility. Its exhausting."

Chelsea squealed in delight. "So just dump his ass, so we can be done with this. Sophie, you look like shit. I'm so sorry if I'm being brutally honest." She wasn't sorry, she was always brutally honest. "The guy's a jealous, insecure a-hole that makes you feel like this." She gestured to my entire person. *Funny how a person's judgements are so easily influenced.* What Chels didn't know was that I was just as possessive and jealous. I was an insecure asshole in my own right.

I had been shattered into a million fragments, and the little gumption I had left within myself was dwindling away at an alarming rate. It frightened me; *everything frightened me.* I tried to keep face, but it was a futile attempt to cover up my own demise; there was no stopping it. I was just trying to contain the impending implosion—methodically distributing each strenuous demand, each volatile confrontation, each emotionally trying situation into minuscule, manageable nooks within myself, hoping at least I would spare those around me.

"I know what you're saying, but you know how difficult it was last time I tried to leave him. He wouldn't fuckin' leave. What am I supposed to do? Move away? We're in the same college and I have to see him everyday anyway." Just saying the words themselves made me feel hopeless.

I had tried to break things off last year. We had been fighting relentlessly about everything and nothing at all. He would ask me why I was wearing thin-strapped shirts—*was I trying to get another guy's attention?* He said I didn't love him and that no one would stay with me once they knew how disgusting of a human being I was—how intolerable I was to live with. I, in turn, told him to shut the fuck up, that he was a sorry excuse for a man, and that he was just a big fake. Everyone might love him, but I knew the truth. He was an insecure hypocrite of a man, he was just better than me at hiding it. *I aimed to hurt*—I retaliated against the truths I heard coming from his mouth.

After one of these arguments, I stormed off in my car to go hang out at the river with Chelsea and Kyle. We drank beers and smoked cigarettes until the early morning. I tried to drown the incessant chatter in my head telling me that I was just a piece of shit. I was no good, unlovable, and so damaged that I would never, ever be capable of mending something I'd never even had: a sense of self.

I returned to my place in the wee hours of the morning exhausted and drunk, only to find that he was still there, sleeping on my futon. I stared at him in his slumber and wondered why I just couldn't make nice. I searched within myself for any part me that was willing to be loved. *For once, Sophie, can't you just get it right*? He just wouldn't leave. He wanted to make things work—*he loved me* . . .

So, at the first glimpse of opportunity, I disappeared like a shadow melting into air. My attempt at redeeming my soul's demise, alas, was to no avail. With my inevitable failure, I proceeded to punish myself with self-demeaning actions that proved Elijah's convictions about me. I needed to lose myself in the chaos of sex and amplified promiscuity, to be enthralled by my prowess in seduction. I was searching for some control, some power. I was trying to feel something other than the excruciating pain my entire being felt. I was attempting to fill a void that was bottomless.

***

Chelsea stopped in her tracks and stepped in front of me. “Ya, Soph. Maybe you should just grab your shit and move out.” She stared earnestly at me. “I’ll help, and we will find you a place. If need be, you are always welcome to move into my parents’ house until you find yourself a suitable apartment.”

I could see the entire scenario playing out in her mind. It was a plausible solution—after all, I was pretty damned good at running away. *At least I used to be.*

Chels walked into our class, leaving me behind to ponder the idea. She had planted a seed, and we both knew it would grow into a palpable plan eventually. Now, only time would tell how long it would take me to get there . . .

“So, I want you guys to take a minute to read over this quote, and then we will have a discussion about its relation—if any—to the type of work you will be performing later on.” The professor patiently waited for everyone to settle down and proceed as instructed.

“Leaders must be close enough to relate to others, but far enough ahead to motivate them.” —John C. Maxwell

“Sophie, would you like to share your thoughts?” The professor stood motionless, awaiting an answer.

“I believe this could easily be associated with the work we will do pertaining to any type of client within the institutions. We must be capable of empathizing with their own unique situations so that we can then create intervention plans that are appropriate for each individual case, and/or issues we are trying to address. We must attempt to foresee possible resistance and plan out how we will go about it. Our job is to show them a path and to try and be proactive in guiding them on that path. Hence, leadership. We must also be capable of knowing when we cannot help in the correct manner, and therefore make the proper decision for the client to be referred to a professional who would be apt to deal with the specific issue," I answered astutely. *Why can't I always perform this well?*

My peers listened attentively, formatting their own replies in their minds, awaiting their time to speak.

"Well done, Sophie." The professor flashed a small grin, seemingly pleased with the opening conversation of the class.

This particular professor always began his classes with quotes that made us think. That was one thing I loved about him, and the reason I preferred his classes the most. He allowed me a chance to think about things more deeply. Opening classes this way gave me a moment to contemplate ideas that I wouldn't normally be thinking about, and it allowed me to see things as possibilities of something greater than myself. Sometimes, I was able to dig a little deeper, and other times, his quotes were provocative and challenged me; it was refreshingly pleasant.

"But," the professor continued, "can anyone tell me—do you believe that you could be a successful worker if you did *not* have empathy for the client? Can you have empathy for an offender who has committed a heinous crime? Do you believe in rehabilitation? These are the questions we shall be discussing today. We will also talk about how we will go about separating our personal issues from our work, so we can be effective in our field."

I relished in the focus that was demanded of me. Directing my mind toward my studies allowed me to detach from my personal dilemmas. I took my education as a challenge. I needed to convince myself that I would amount to something—*anything.* Also, I wanted to prove to everyone else that when I said I would do something, I would do it. The showing-the-world-they-were-wrong type of thing.

I thought of Principal B, my high school principal. On the day of my high school graduation, while she was handing me my diploma, she looked at me square in the eye and said, *I didn't think you could make it.* I withheld the temptation to spit in her face. Although the action would have gratified my defiance, I somehow couldn't shake the feeling that I would always be a failure . . . unless . . . *unless what?*

I clung to the idea that I would be transformed once I had a title and a set path to follow. I was praying to God that I would find redemption at the end of this road. I prayed that I would be spared an entire adulthood of insurmountable obstacles, seeing as how I had overpaid my dues—*hadn't I?* I was now at least trying harder than I ever had to make something of myself, yet I knew that deep down, my self-sabotage was quite vicious. I knew I would need to slay her like the two-headed dragon she was.

CHAPTER 5

"Its nice to see you again, Sophie Ann." His tone denoted a slight annoyance, probably at my lack of accountability toward my therapy. Rightfully so, as he was the one who had to re-adjust his schedule every single time I didn't show up. It took patience and perseverance on his part to continue to work with me. I appreciated the effort, even though I didn't say it out loud. At least one person wasn't giving up on me so easily.

"Hey Paul, I must admit I kinda missed your face," I smiled cowedly. "I'm sorry. I've been a total mess as per usual. Therefore, I've been avoiding you." I crossed my legs and leaned against the arm rest, preparing myself for the oncoming freight train that would more then likely appear during the session.

"I see. Well, would you like to elaborate as to why you've been avoiding your therapy sessions?" He mimicked my body posture.

I inhaled deeply. "Well, all in this short time span, I've managed to throw myself back into this shitty relationship with Elijah, I've been avoiding my mother like the plague, end-semester exams are coming up, and after that, I know I'll have to make some sort of move, on top of being fully available for my practicum demands. It's a lot of responsibility and it's causing my anxiety to flare up." I squirmed in my seat.

"I see. There's lots happening here, Sophie. It's understandable that you may be feeling the pressure quite a bit. All this stress, per se, seems proportional to the situations present. What would you like to talk about first? Would you like to address the struggles with Elijah or your mother? Or, we could speak about the demands of your school? It's up to you." He waited patiently for me to gather my thoughts.

"None of the above . . . is that an option?" I tested. I didn't wait for him to reply. I cleared my throat and began.

I had to begin somewhere.

"I honestly was feeling pitiful about myself, and then Elijah came around. Somehow, he could sense that I was feeling weak, and he took advantage of the situation—I let him take advantage . . . I'm very aware of the predicament I put myself in. I just couldn't help but to indulge in my self-sabotage, you know, because that's what I do. And I do it very fuckin' well. He made me feel so good for the first few weeks, as usual. I made him feel so good, too. As soon as things get too "normal," I freak out. I don't know how to handle this type of shit. It feels wrong . . . *I can see her within myself—I see Elijah through her eyes* . . . Am I fuckin' crazy?! Now it's like a python is slowly slithering around my entire being and increasing the pressure all-so-slightly that you barely notice it . . . until one day you just fall asleep and you never wake up again, and it would probably be easier that way anyway than to face the drama that all this shit is going to lead to." I looked at him with great affliction.

He nodded his head but remained silent.

I continued. "My mother has been drinking more and more this past year; or maybe its because now I am aware that it's abnormal to drink that much. Anyway, I'm struggling. I'm struggling because I can't do anything about it. She won't listen to me. She avoids the topic of her alcoholism. Wow! I don't think I've ever said that out loud to anyone before." I caught myself by surprise with the realization that I had never verbalized this description of my mother until this day.

I continued, "I honestly think that she thinks she doesn't even have a problem. It's not cool anymore, you know? Everywhere we go—family gatherings, Christmas parties, barbecues—everyone is silently staring and placing their judgment on her. They whisper to one another when she begins to get drunk. I see them. Somehow, she doesn't. It makes me sick to witness their sense of superiority and disgust toward her, and so I just follow along and drink too, so at least she's not alone, you know? At least when everyone's gone I can still look at myself and say, *hey, at least you weren't one of them.*"

The tears flowed down my cheeks like the cascade of a waterfall, ruthless and incessant. "I can't fathom a future where I haven't the ability to self-inflict my own demise, out of shame that I may one day look at her like *they* do. How fucked up is that? I'm afraid to be more—to be better, to feel—because she hasn't gotten there yet. I'm still waiting on her to come around, to be my guidance, but I know it won't happen." My eyes remained focused on my hands. The little girl within shuddered as the words escaped my mouth.

"The further I advance in my degree, the more I realize how fucked up my life has been; how almost everything was abnormal. No wonder I've never been able to steadily stand in this world. You know?" My voice quivered. "I search for the next thing that can make me feel—feel anything. Whether it's the drugs, the sex, the booze, or shitty relationships. I'm always looking for relief—somewhere out there, because I can't find it in here." I tapped my chest.

"On top of that, I'm doing my final practicum in a young offenders' facility, where most of these kids come from homes exactly like mine. Except I had too many responsibilities to handle, and I wouldn't dare leave my mother alone to fend for herself. And here I am: Twenty-one years old and still fucked up. Maybe even more so, yet I chose to get a degree where I have to look into the eyes of all these kids, and tell them what?" My voice raised into a shout. The rage, the injustice, the self-loathing pity erupted out of every pore in my body.

"What the fuck am I to do now, Paul? You tell me. Because I can't and won't go around telling these young, hostile, terrified, damaged kids that it's gonna be all right. What if it's not?"

I leaned over, hugged my knees, and sobbed. The pain, the release, the mixture of accumulated emotions, finally had somewhere safe to be expressed. The whirlwind of emotions spun around me like a cyclone swallowing everything in its trajectory.

When I finally looked up through my blurred, stinging eyes, Paul handed me a box of tissues and a glass of water. He cleared his throat and began.

"Sophie, I think you and I both know that you have taken it upon yourself to carry many burdens that do not belong to you. I think that when the time comes, you will be able to finally release your feelings of encumbrance toward the decisions your mother makes."

I listened attentively.

"Because of your upbringing and the circumstances of many of your life's traumatic events, you have found a way to "deal" with what was happening by not focusing on you. You put all your focus onto others and fixate on your need to protect them. This has been your survival mechanism—this has been your lifeline. Your memories from a very early age are of traumatic impact. You still suffer from what I suspect to be post-traumatic stress disorder that has never been addressed seriously until now. Depression is also an ongoing issue. You just seem to have a very high tolerance for it, and an ability to camouflage its effects within yourself while you are surrounded by others. You are the billboard of a functioning woman with a mental health disorder.

I swallowed hard. I had never been summed up like that before. I could mentally see the DSM-V, all the check marks I'd collected under each disorder, and how they determined who I was. The thought that I was all these things mortified me.

"Sophie, there are many factors behind why you do what you do today. You are not a bad person because of the things you do, you are a person with an invisible illness. I also believe that is why you chose to work in this field. You are extraordinarily resilient, and I am amazed at how seemingly well you have fared, considering. This will be a long journey from here, Sophie—just like when you work with the kids, we will make a therapeutic plan on how to find the proper coping mechanisms and tools for your day-to-day life, and continue to work together in therapy to alleviate the weight you have carried alone for all these years." He placed his hands on my knee and gently tapped it.

"You are not alone anymore, and there is nothing to be ashamed of. Everyone has different coping mechanisms. We just need to find you some that aren't so self-destructive. I have seen a great change in your impulsive reactions since you have been on your antidepressants and in therapy. They seem to have helped greatly to stabilize your fight-or-flight mode and your anxiety spells." He leaned back in his chair.

"I won't lie and tell you that this is as hard as it's gonna get . . . *but*, I will tell you that you are finally giving yourself a fighting chance for your ideal life. You have much to give this world. I want you to know that you're filled with unlimited potential. This is just the beginning." He smiled slightly, resonating a sincere sentiment toward me.

It gave me a feeling of warmth.

My eyes throbbed and burned from the tears. I could taste their saltiness as I licked my lips. I understood what he was telling me, I just felt so isolated, *alone.* I was tired of being brave, being angry, and being the one who seemed to be so tough that people joked about it. Most people just made fun of my angry disposition and laughed it off as a façade. I was tired . . .

"I know, Paul." My voice was weak and my throat was dry from the sobbing. "So what now?"

"I suggest you take a leap of faith and go to the Al-Anon meetings that happen about three times a week at different locations near here. It will give you a chance to find a support group—a place where you can hear other stories that resonate with you—and maybe you'll find the strength to reach out in due time. Al-Anon is a wonderful resource that I suggest you utilize in conjunction with our therapy sessions." He handed me the information booklet.

"I believe you already know that your relationship with Elijah is a toxic one. If it is not beneficial to your healing, then maybe you should consider the choices that are appropriate for *your* well-being."

I exhaled heavily. My body was depleted of all energy.

"Thirdly, we will continue your sessions every other week from now on. If you agree, I think you would benefit from more frequent sessions, as I think they will help you advance. What do you think?" He waited patiently, his fingers interconnected and placed lightly on his crossed knee.

"Ya, I'll come every other week. And I'll consider Al-Anon. I'm not a fan of crying my sob story in front of others—except you, of course." I smiled. I had regained some of my sarcastic sense of humor and ill-placed pride. "But I want to quit my meds." I cleared my throat. The conversation made me uncomfortable. I had an obligation toward myself to be transparent with him.

"I have an appointment with the doctor in a few days. They make me drowsy and I can't focus on my schooling . . ." I shifted in my chair uneasily. "I've been consuming stuff every now and then."

He waited.

"Okay, I'm consuming a shitload, but I'm trying to reel myself in. Anyway, I don't want to make things worse—I'm actually trying to find a way to make it work. I've already decided, so that's that." I awaited his reply, knowing he would not like my cessation of my antidepressants. All I knew was that I didn't like how they made me feel, and how they didn't make me feel.

"I cannot tell you whether or not that is what you need to do, but please make sure you have a plan set up by the doctor to help you take the proper steps to come off your meds. Coming off of antidepressants too quickly can be very harmful, even dangerous. So, please follow through with the doctor's recommendations." He stared intently, pausing for a long moment to make his point quite clear. "As far as the matter of your self-medication, that is another topic we will begin to address as the therapy continues. For the time being, try to follow the doctor's recommendations. Please, Sophie."

"I sure will," I retorted.

***

It was eight o'clock when I pulled up to the church. I parked my car under the buzzing streetlight and sat there looking like I was holding a stakeout, trying to gather my gumption before I exited. Isn't this how all horror movies start? A girl walks into a poorly lit basement entrance, expecting to meet someone or looking for something, and then all of a sudden, she's captured and dragged to the torment chambers where the unthinkable occurs, and she simply dies from sheer fear. I hoped this was not the way I was going to die. It probably wasn't, but the thought of sitting in a room full of strangers bawling their eyes out seemed equally terrifying. I'll admit the horror movie scenario was far-fetched, but it was plausible. Okay, maybe slightly melodramatic, but still plausible.

Ready or not, here I go.

The building was eerily silent and dimly lit. *Why did they have to make things so unwelcoming?* It had taken everything I had in me to show up—if not for myself, then for the fact that I could finally show Paul that I was making real efforts at not sucking at life and wallowing in self-pity. *See, I could be a good girl too.*

I entered the room, where a table that would have been long enough to welcome the twelve disciples greeted me. There were six or seven others already present, silently talking amongst one another. They all fell silent when they noticed me. The man sitting at the end of table stood up and came to greet me.

"Welcome." He shook my hand. "I'm Richard, the facilitator for this Al-Anon group. What's your name?" He looked at me endearingly.

I stood there, mortified. Was he really expecting me to speak publicly? I was hoping to just sneak in, sit in, and leave—not actually share.

"I'm Sophie," I squeaked.

"Well, it's our pleasure to have you join us, Sophie. Thank you." Richard walked me to the table. "You can sit anywhere you'd like. We are just about to begin, but before we do, I will grab you a welcome packet."

I sat in the chair closest to the door, hoping that I would have first dibs on the exit if ever some lunatic decided to crash our little get-together. *Safety first.*

Richard brought me the welcome packet, and I thanked him. Then, he sat back down. Once he did, everyone became silent, anticipating the next step. I sat there clueless, looking for minutes, or something I could follow.

The group began:

God, grant me the serenity to accept the things I cannot change, the courage to change the things I can, and the wisdom to know the difference. Amen.

"Amen," I added.

"Today we welcome a new soul to our table. Please give the space for this individual to gather the courage and to receive the information that is necessary for her to heal." Richard spoke so eloquently.

Everyone looked at me. "Welcome, Sophie," they said as a chorus.

"So, is there anyone who would like to share?" he asked.

Everyone looked around the room, politely waiting for the first person to pronounce themselves. I sat there noticing that I was the only person there who was under forty. I felt a sinking feeling. I wanted to flee, but my pride was stronger, and it forced me to sit tight.

A beautiful, tired-looking woman spoke first. "Well, Jerry's been binging a lot lately. He disappeared for several days without any news. I thought he was dead," her voice quivered. "I finally had enough and decided to move out, until he gets help. I've been asking him for fifteen years to get help, and I've only now realized that if I stick around, I will just continue to encourage his behavior, because it's too hard for me to see him getting sick and angry and volatile. So, I always cave in. I found myself a little apartment in the next borough, far enough from him and near the canal. It has a great view, and the market is close enough that I can walk there." She began to cry.

Everyone sat there silently, seemingly unfazed by the display of agony this woman was expressing. Richard slid the Kleenex box over to her but remained quiet. I began to squirm in my chair. *Wasn't anyone gonna say something?* This poor woman. I could feel a lump tighten in my throat.

"I told him we were done, until he finally addressed the issue. Now, I'm terrified that my marriage is actually over, because he loves the bottle more than he loves me," she sobbed.

After a minute of silently listening to her sob, Richard cleared his throat. "Thank you for sharing. We are here for you." He placed his hand over hers and gave it a gentle squeeze.

"Thank you, Monique," everyone piped in.

Was that really it? They love the bottle more than they love us?

***

"Mother, please turn down your music, I'm trying to sleep here!" I shouted from my bedroom. I lay in bed waiting for her to get up and turn the volume down . . . but she didn't.

I'd finally had enough. I got up, stormed out of my room, and went to do it myself.

"You could show some respect, hey? I have school in the morning!" I shouted as I entered the room.

She and her friends were sitting around the table, smoking and drinking. Her friends sat silently, waiting for her to reply.

"Go to bed and just *suck it up*!" she spat.

I stormed away into my room, slamming the door behind me. The anger and shame vibrated within me. I placed my pillow over my head and tried to drown the noise. When I left for school the next morning, after having barely slept, I found them all sprawled out across the apartment. Wherever they had landed, that's where they had fallen asleep.

They had also forgotten to clean up the baggies of cocaine in the bathroom . . .

***

There were a few more stories told during the meeting that evening. Each one seemed more trying than the next. All these people loved someone who was an alcoholic, and each one suffered because they loved that alcoholic. For some of them, it was their children; for others, it was their spouse. For me, it was my alcoholic mother, but I didn't doubt that my story was like all the others: it was heart-wrenching.

To love someone who is an alcoholic is like living in a perpetual emotional roller coaster from hell.

When the meeting ended, I felt exhausted. The emotions in the room were palpable, and the entire room was filled with sorrow. I stood, feeling light-headed.

"Thank you for sitting with us today, Sophie. We truly hope you come back and maybe share your story with us, when you feel comfortable enough." Richard shook my hand. "We wish you well."

"Thank you," I replied.

I drove home thinking about that woman, Monique, and the courage it must have taken for her to face her husband—the man she had shared her life with—and leave him. Not because she had lost her love for him, but because somewhere along the way, she realized she needed to love herself a little more.

Maybe one day I would find that courage.

Maybe one day I could and would be brave, too...

***

I had cleaned my apartment and my bags were set beside the door in the sunroom, where Elijah would run into them when he arrived after his classes. I had decided to take the day off and clear my head. During that head-clearing, I had also decided that I would take a few days to myself and go to the mountains to visit my mother. I needed the quiet and the comfort I was hoping to find by going back home.

I missed her.

The more I spoke openly about myself with Paul, the more I realized that speaking was the only way I would actually face all the things I had repressed. The thought alone made my stomach leap into my mouth;

the vertigo intensifying as though I were standing at the top of the highest diving board, terrified of making the jump.

You can do this, Sophie. You're full of moxie, remember?

I sat at my bistro table engulfed by my cigarette smoke while staring out the window to the icy river below. The frozen landscape resembled the stillness found in the tundra, ceding to the illusion that it bore no life. In reality, the placidity was merely a deception of the naked eye. Under the snow and ice roared a river so powerful it could sweep you two miles down in the blink of an eye.

He stomped his feet against the door frame to remove the excess snow before entering. I sat erect, awaiting the inevitable interrogation. The rhythm of my heart accelerated. I knew I had to put aside my vulnerability and prepare to assert my desire to be alone.

As he turned around, closing the door behind him, he saw my bags. His breathing paused. Then, he turned and looked at me. "Where the hell have you been today?" His tone was berating. He towered over me. I awaited the lengthy questioning session he was ramping up to.

"I had an appointment this morning and then I didn't feel like going to class," I said matter-of-factly.

He stood, annoyed with my short answer. I could sense the frustration and anger building within him. "An appointment where? With who? You never told me about this."

"I forgot I had one until this morning. It's not a big deal. I only had two classes today anyway, so what's your problem?" I leaned back and lit another cigarette, breathing in the nicotine to alleviate my rising panic.

I hated these confrontations, yet I couldn't help but propel myself into them. I hadn't forgotten about my appointment, and yes, I had pre-meditated the omission because I didn't want Elijah to be aware of what I was doing. I was ashamed of myself and I also wanted to succeed—all at the same time.

"Okay there, Sophie." His voice was condescending as he rolled his eyes.

"Look, I don't want to get into this with you. Really, I just want to have some space." I stood up, hoping that I would feel bigger by doing so. "I'm going Up North for a few days and I'm gonna spend some time thinking about stuff." My heart began to pound in my chest. I tried to reel myself back to avoid the mess.

I could sense his anger rising; his questioning mind quickly unfurled a thousand scenarios of *why* I was leaving and *what* I would be doing. I could imagine that each new scenario was worse than its precedent. His cheeks flushed. He dropped his bags on the ground and gathered himself as he processed the words I had spoken.

"Look Soph. I know it's been rocky, but baby, come on. You don't have to go." He had chosen to take the smooth route to try and divert my plan. He walked closer to me, coaxing, every step swallowing the minute amount of air I was capable of forcing myself to inhale. "Come on. If you want to get away, then why don't I come with you?" He stroked my arm with the back of his fingers. "We can go anywhere you want—together."

"I don't want you to come with me." I moved away from him and walked further into the apartment. "I need some space. I *want* some space."

He followed. "Come on. I haven't been back to your mom's since last year. It could be nice to try and bond, ya know." He was slithering like a snake in the grass.

"Elijah, I'm going Up North ALONE. Plus, my mother doesn't like you. You already know this. I don't want to . . ." I grabbed myself a glass of water to alleviate my parched throat.

"Fine, Sophie. You go Up North to *visit your mother*. I know what you're up to. You're gonna go see that ex-boss of yours and fuck him." I shuddered as his words struck.

His vile slander had finally surfaced. I had anticipated his reaction. I should have left before he arrived, but I wanted to own up to what I wanted. I needed to proclaim my right to stand up for myself.

"Fuck you, Elijah. Fuck you." I walked back to the sunroom to grab my jacket. As I swung it around my back to put it on, Elijah caught it.

"Give me my jacket, Elijah. Don't be an asshole," I said with as much calmness as I could muster.

"I'm not letting you go until you tell me the truth. Are you going back to fuck that guy?" He clenched his teeth, awaiting a response—*any response.*

I lost my composure and lunged at him. My hand collided with his face. The stinging pain of the impact shot through my palm. He barely flinched, expecting this outcome. He puffed out his chest like a gorilla claiming his authority. His giant hand wrapped around my wrist as he pulled me back into the apartment and shoved me into the next room. He closed the French door—the door that led to my escape. He placed his body in front of it in defiance.

My mind raced; my instincts flared up. I tried to process the best way to get myself from this side of the door back to the other side. Everything I had learned during my program flooded my mind.

Fuck, fuck, fuck. Remain calm, Sophie, remain calm. Get yourself out of this situation. Don't panic. Don't instigate. Don't provoke.

But every part of my existence was telling me to fight this asshole. How dare he control whether or not I got to leave?

Admit it, you enjoy the chaos, you thrive in this shit.

So, without much resistance to relapsing so quickly into old habits, I pounced on him like the ferocious lioness I had grown up to become. I pushed him back into the wall, throwing him off balance. With my surprise attack successfully executed, I attempted to grab him and pull him out from in front of the door—but this attempt came up short. He had planted his feet and leaned his body against the door handle. My bid proved futile, I hoped he would come after me.

"Come on Elijah, what are you gonna do?!" I shouted at him. "Come on, hit me, you asshole!" There they finally were; those famous words came tumbling out of my mouth. I refrained my shock because of senseless pride, but there it was. The vicious cycle had reached the beginning—*I had finally crossed the line.*

Elijah took two steps to reach me. "Shut the fuck up Sophie, I ain't gonna hit you!"

I walked around him and made my way back to the door. With one swift motion, he released my jacket with the fling of his wrist.

"Take your shit and just go, then!" he screamed.

I screeched when the weight of my phone and keys collided with my head, temporarily knocking me into a dizzy spell.

"What the fuck is your problem? You look like a fuckin' crazy bitch!" he shouted, shocked about what had happened. "Why would you do this?! Why would you make a scene? You're so fucked up, Sophie. Look what you did!" His breath was sporadic, his mouth pasty. A glob of white phlegm stuck to the side of his mouth and teeth as he spoke, making him resemble a rabid creature.

I hunched over and held my head in my hands. The throbbing rose to its pinnacle as the blood rushed to the point of impact, creating an immediate bruise. My heart protruded from my temples, each beat seemingly trying to escape my head. I looked up at him with rage. "You fuckin' piece of shit! Look what I DID?! How about you look at what YOU did!" I gritted my teeth. "You've made a scene loud enough that I won't be surprised if the cops show up." I stood up straight, gaining back my authoritative stance. *Playing out this scene as easily as my mother would have.*

"You like to make things look like you're the victim, Sophie," he spewed, "but you're not. You push and you push. It's like you want this terrifying story to tell. I ain't gonna fall for your shit! You're so fucked up!" Cries of anger and sadness came crashing out of his steel blue eyes.

He wasn't wrong.

He threw his hands in the air and sat himself down. I picked up my jacket and put it on. "You're going to look really cute if the cops do show up. What's that gonna look like for you?" I stared at him, threatening.

"You're the assailant and I would be able to prove that. Look at my arms." He pointed to the scratches and blood that covered a portion of his forearms.

I laughed.

As I opened the door to the sunroom, I looked over my shoulder to deliver my final message. "I want you to find a place to move. This is my apartment, not yours. I'm sick of this shit. I'M DONE!" I shouted.

I grabbed my bags and stormed out before he had a chance to reply. I got to my car and hopped in, putting it in gear and speeding off before I had buckled up. The tears of anger and frustration spilled out of my eyes, making the drive indistinct. I made it a mile down the back roads before pulling over. I opened the door to my car and leaned out to vomit. The stress and panic I had put myself through were finally surfacing. After the initial vomiting episode, I stayed slouched over, dry-heaving for a few minutes. Once assured that I was completely done, I fell back into my seat and sobbed. The swells of lament came and went like the steady flow of the tide. I allowed my body to dissolve in tears. I surrendered to the agony within, knowing I didn't have to hide from anyone. The shame and torment that I put myself through . . . I didn't even understand how things had gotten this way. My brain didn't think. I became possessed by this uncontrollable urge to plummet into chaos and along the way, I dragged down anyone I could along with me. Why were things the way that they were, and would I ever change?

I had crossed the line. I had finally surfaced the demons that hid within me. Unknown to myself, I had recreated everything I had ever known. *I was the creator of my own demise . . .*

After what seemed like an eternity, I finally regained my composure. I dabbed my eyes and flinched when my sleeve grazed the side of my temple.

"Ah, shit," I squinted. "I'm gonna need to hide this," I said to myself as I examined the aftermath.

I fiddled with my hair, trying to get it to cover the bruise that was already showing. I just couldn't get it right. The frustration began surfacing again. "Dammit!" I shouted to my reflection.

I reached over to the passenger seat and dumped out the entire contents of my purse in search of my concealer. I found it and meticulously began to apply the magic serum. Once my work was complete, I sat back, as satisfied as I would be with the end result. I turned the key in the ignition and made my way back to the highway that would lead me home.

CHAPTER 6

I could see the varying hues of gray and white smoke emitting from the chimney before the house itself entered my line of sight. One short bend further and there she was—solace. The incandescent, golden glow of the reading lamps emanated through the windows and scintillated against the snow.

As I made my way to the house, the crunching of the packed snow under my boots echoed through the darkened forest and reverberated off the surface of the frozen lake. I inhaled the frigid mountain air, my lungs instantly exploding with vigor that shot through my entire being. I was finally able to release the tension I had been holding in my shoulders for the past three hours. I silently prayed that mother would offer me a safe haven while I picked myself up.

From the entrance, I could see directly into the living room by the glow of several dim nighttime lights. No one was in sight, but I could sense that the house was still awake. I carefully deposited my bags and made my way toward the vivid, crackling fire. As I got closer, the heat caressed my face as softly as a warm embrace welcoming me home.

"Sophie. You're home." She stood up from the floor. I hadn't seen her from where I was standing.

"Mom!" I cried.

She gathered me in her arms and we held each other as though I had just returned from a long voyage. It *had been* a long voyage since the last time I had been home. I melted into the familiar scent that was her. She appeased my heavy heart simply by her embrace. Only in her arms could I crumble and allow the little girl within to show her fragility. I often had to be the nurturer—the one who had to oversee our overall well-being, the one who made sure we didn't drown in our own recklessness. But sometimes, she would take back the reigns and allow me to be a child. This was one of those moments. It was as though she knew, before I even happened to show up, that I would need her.

In times like these, things were just as they were supposed to be. A mother comforting her child—safe.

"Sweetie, what's going on?" She tried to pull away so she could get a better look at me, but I held on tight. *Please don't let me go*, I wanted to shout. She didn't resist, nor question the action, so we stood in our embrace for a long time.

"I'm sorry I showed up without announcing," I said coyly. I didn't want to spew all the unbearable happenings I had put myself through within the first fifteen minutes of being home.

"Don't be ridiculous, Sophie. You show up here whenever the hell you want to, this is your home, too," she scolded.

As she spoke those words, my tears unexpectedly swelled to the surface. I swallowed sharply.

She stood back, narrowing her stare. She tilted her head as she analyzed the situation as thoroughly as a trained sniper—always ready and alert, assessing possible threats and taking down the menace as swiftly as possible.

"So. What's the problem? I know *you*. There's something going on that you haven't been telling me." She sat back down on the ground, where she was swarmed in tiny pieces of different fabrics, along with a slew of staples and sheers.

"What are you up to? You found yourself a new piece of antique to refurbish?" I attempted to divert the conversation.

"Smooth, child, but I am not so easily swayed. But yes, I did find this really cute piece that I just *had* to bring back to life. Can you believe that people throw stuff like this away—it's crazy," she stated excitedly.

I sat down beside her and played with the pieces that lay around us. She was amazingly skilled in so many different things. *Why hadn't she ever given herself a chance?* She liked to call herself a Jill-of-all-trades, which was an accurate representation of her abilities. I could see only two beer bottles beside her, and one of them was still half-full. She must have been very preoccupied with the task at hand to suspend her need to drink. Alcoholics don't *want* a drink, they *need* a drink.

I could sense that she was waiting for me to begin.

"I have had a lot on my plate this semester" I began, "and I haven't always been feeling super-great." I minimized the intensity of my despair, trying fruitlessly to remove myself from the quicksand I had fallen into.

She leaned against the wood pile and picked up her beer.

"Anyway, so because of all that, I resumed my therapy sessions with Paul. And that's been helping me, but I also decided to come off my antidepressants, which Paul doesn't think is a decision I should take lightly." I got up and went to sit closer to the warmth of the fireplace, hoping the shivering in my body would cease. I lit myself a cigarette.

"Okay, so did you go see your doctor and talk about coming off of them?" she asked gently. "Because when you were younger and we had you on them, it took quite a while to reduce the dosage. You did mention that, right?"

"Ya, I did. I'm just so frustrated that it's going to take so long. I don't want to be on them anymore. I really don't think I *need* them, either. They're making my ability to focus in class really hard, Mom." I could feel the urgency and panic rise in my chest. The conversation was getting me all riled up. I tried to justify my choices.

"Sweetie, its okay. You don't need to justify yourself." She had read my mind. She placed her hand on my knee and as she drew in closer, she noticed the discoloration on my temple.

"What the hell is *that*?" Her eyes widened. I could see her tensing up, readying herself to hear the scenario she had already played out in her mind before I even had time to open my mouth.

"It's nothing, really." I knew I couldn't dance around it much longer, so I decided it would be best if I just came out and told her that I had started dating Elijah again.

"Elijah and I started dating again, not long after we returned to classes." I paused and took a deep drag. The crackling sound of the cigarette slowly retracting resonated in my ears.

"And he moved right back in and things just don't *fit,* him and I. I didn't ask him to move back, but I didn't state my preferences, either. So, anyway, I guess I'm as much to blame in all of this, you know? We got into a pretty big fight before I left, and I sorta pushed his buttons and so this happened—it was an accident. My keys and phone were in my coat pocket . . . but maybe it wouldn't have happened if I wouldn't have launched myself at him and got up in his face. I'm just as much of an ass as he is. In reality, I can say that maybe that's what I wanted him to do." I stopped, waiting for her reaction. I had finally reached that place—I had become a reflection of her. I *was* her.

"Well, that's just fuckin' cute, isn't it?" She clenched her jaw. "I told you last year, Sophie, I don't like that boy. There's something about him that just ain't right. He's got some hidden demons. And don't get me started on his eyes." She closed her eyes tightly.

What about my demons? I thought.

She took a big swig of her beer, and afterward, she was surprisingly calm. Her outrage had reeled in. It took me aback, but I was deeply relieved that I didn't have to navigate her highly sensitive, easily offended, capricious feelings. I could just let myself stew in my own crisis for once.

She came to me and cradled me in her arms, coaxing me to lay my head on her lap. As she began to stroke my hair with the tenderness and nurturing only a mother could give, I reluctantly allowed myself to dissolve in the outpour of my pain. I lay there unwilling and unable to move my depleted self from the ground. As we had so many times before, only with roles reversed, we sat on the floor, silently; riding out the assault, weeping for one another's pain. The pain somehow always intertwined within us, and the vines embedded themselves into the deepest depths of the earth.

"I'm exhausted, Mom." The tears had finally subsided, and I no longer had the energy to produce any more. I didn't know that was even possible.

As I pushed myself up to my knees, my mother's jade and steel blue eyes sparkled with a clarity and resolution I had not witnessed for a long time. She took my hand.

"Okay, sweetie, you go on up to bed and get a good night's rest. You'll feel better in the morning, and we can talk some more about it then." She squeezed me tightly.

"Thanks for being there, Mom. I love you." I squeezed her back and got up to put myself to bed, barely capable of seeing my trajectory due to the swelling of my eyes from all the crying I'd been doing. I maneuvered through the house and up the stairs to my room. I bypassed the bathroom and collapsed into my bed, where I found sleep the instant my head landed on the pillow.

***

The tantalizing smell of breakfast awoke me from a deep and heavy sleep. I slowly turned toward the window and allowed my eyes to adjust to the brightness of the morning rays peeking through the tree branches. It took me a minute to register where I was, but only a second to have the events of the previous day come flooding back. I pushed them aside, refusing to open up that dam. I turned my focus to the shadows that danced upon my blankets, tracing them with my fingertips. The thoughtless motion instantly appeased my drifting mind.

"You're gonna get up and you're gonna suck it up," I said to myself. And with that, I resolutely followed the delicious smell.

I found her working away in the kitchen. She looked like a little busy bee buzzing from one place to the next. "Wow, Mom. What's the feast for?" I approached her and wrapped my arms around her back as she prepared my cup of coffee.

"Good morning, sleepyhead." She smiled and handed me a scorching-hot, blessed cup of coffee.

"You are the best. I could get used to this," I said jokingly.

"You mean you *are* used to this, because I've always spoiled you, child." She smiled sweetly.

I appreciated the nurturing she was bestowing upon me. She had a big heart and a powerful love for her children.

"You still look tired, sweetie. Did you manage to sleep at all?" she questioned.

"Oh ya, all that crying made me fall asleep right away. It was kinda nice. I just feel like I have a heavy head, and like I got punched in the face." I smiled. "Look at my eyes, for crying out loud. I could be transforming into a frog any minute now, with them bulging like that," I whined.

She laughed. "Oh, you're silly." She swatted my arm and pulled my cheek. "You're cute regardless of your frog eyes," she said in a teasing voice.

It made me smile.

"Here, grab your plate. I made all of your favorite stuff, so let's eat." She took a warm plate out of the oven and handed it to me. It was filled with French toast and scrambled eggs, a side of bacon, fresh fruit, and a small bowl of beans.

We sat down, both of us choosing chairs that faced the lake. Even though it was winter, we loved being in the presence of the water. Unconsciously, we probably knew the symbolism of its purifying properties. It may have been the reason why we were drawn to it with such yearning.

"So, how did you sleep? You look rested, I must say," I remarked. I had scanned the kitchen for any traces of abandoned corpses, but to my surprise, there were none to be found.

"You know I don't sleep," she said matter-of-factly. "What is sleep?" she snorted.

"Well, whatever. You look good. Thanks for all of this," I gestured. "I appreciate it, Mom."

"You're welcome, sweetie. So, after breakfast, I want you to go shower and wash the stink off of you. Then you and I are going to do a little shopping." She smiled at me.

"Shopping for what?" I questioned.

"Clothes and whatever else we might want. It's gonna do us some good to have a little girl time—its been so long." She seemed very pleased with her plans.

"Alrighty, I agree. It's gonna do us some good for sure." I was happy she had planned a distraction for the day. If it hadn't been for her, I probably would have moped around the house.

***

I let the warmth of the water cascade down my body, attempting to cleanse the agony. I couldn't release the heaviness I felt within my heart. Why had I let things get this far with Elijah? Why did I feel the need to prove that all my relationships would turn into bad ones? Why wasn't I capable of just moving on? Was there a way out from all this? I wanted to leave, but I was afraid of myself. I wanted to change, but I didn't know if I could. I was tired of always feeling unworthy and terrified of my surroundings everywhere I went, regardless of who I was with or what I was doing. I was always uncomfortable, always uneasy in my own skin . . . as though I were trying to find the exit, a tiny crevice I could crawl out from and shed the skin that never felt as though it belonged to me. Maybe I had accidentally been dropped into this one, and then the Almighty above found out about the horrendous error, but by then it was too late. He could have opted to kill me off so I could begin again, but obviously I was here, so that wasn't how things had played out.

I stood underneath the beating of the water until the temperature began to change. It snapped me out from inside my head and forced me to rush against the quickly cooling water. I finished rinsing my hair as the water became frigid.

I grabbed my towel and shivered as the water dripped from my frozen body, pooling around my feet. I may have been freezing, but that was just what I needed to snap me back. I wiped myself down and got ready for the day ahead.

***

"So what's the plan, Stan?" I asked.

We were on the highway heading toward the city. She was driving with her window half down to let the smoke out. She took a drag.

"We are going to buy ourselves some clothes." The smoke played around her nostrils and out of her mouth as she spoke. "We're gonna find something that makes you feel good. Then, we can eat wherever you want. That's all I have planned."

"Sounds good to me." I sat back and turned up the volume on the radio. Ironically, the song my mother had dedicated to me at my high school graduation was playing: Lee Ann Womack's "I Hope You Dance."

I listened to my mother sing along.

I hope you never fear those mountains in the distance

Never settle for the path of least resistance

Livin' might mean takin' chances, but they're worth takin'

Lovin' might be a mistake, but it's worth makin'

Don't let some hellbent heart leave you bitter

When you come close to sellin' out, reconsider
Give the heavens above more than just a passing glance . . .

The music faded in the background as I sat silently. I inhaled deeply to suppress the lingering pull I felt in my chest. I stared outside the window, watching the scenery fly by, wondering where this life would lead me.

We pulled up to a giant Bed Bath and Beyond storefront. This wasn't the type of shopping I had been told about. "Mom, what are we doing at Bed Bath and Beyond?"

"We are getting *you* some new bedding," she stated.

"I don't need new bedding, Mom. I just bought some a few years ago when I moved to the city," I said, puzzled.

"You always need new bedding when you move into a new place . . . and, always buy a new broom, too," she said matter-of-factly.

I laughed. "Why the hell do you need a new broom if you move to a new place, first of all? And who the hell is moving?" I tried to unravel the hidden agenda she seemed to have pulled out.

"You always buy a new broom because it's bad luck to bring the dust from your previous place to the new one. It's like carrying around all kinds of unwanted attachments. Didn't I ever teach you that?" She looked at me as we entered the giant store.

"I find that hard to believe, but okay. Superstition is a thing, so I guess I'll keep that in mind next time I move. So, who's moving?" I stopped and looked at her quizzically.

"You are."

"What do you mean, *I am*? I already have my own place." Alarm shot through my body. Panic began to rise, making my cheeks boil.

"Sweetie, if there's one thing I know, I know a bad relationship when I see one. And sweetheart, this one is gonna tear you apart if you don't get the hell outta there." Her eyes peered at me with determination. "So, you, my girl, are gonna gather yourself up. Finish your semester and we will go from there," she delivered.

My throat was dry. I could tell she had thoroughly thought out a plan that would lead to my successful escape from a relationship she deemed valueless. I gathered my thoughts as I processed the evident change of my life plan and immediate relationship status. Somehow, she had managed to take my life—albeit not a very happy or conducive to happiness one—and completely remodel it without my input. I was taken aback.

"Mom, what the heck are you talking about? You expect me to just be done, *like that*?" I snapped my fingers. "To be done *like that* with Elijah? You don't know half the story, and that's not even important. But maybe I'm not ready to be done with him. Maybe I want to stick around and suck it up until I graduate from this program so then I can just fuck off to somewhere he won't find me." My anxiety was in full-flare.

She stood quietly while I went on and on. Once I paused, she stared at me. "Are you done having a conniption fit?"

I nodded.

"Well, sweetie, sometimes you just have to face the music and take the shit you've been dealt and run with it. I sure as hell am not gonna stand by and watch you sell yourself short because of you don't want to hurt some boys' feelings."

She walked down the aisles into the kitchen department and stood in front of an array of multicolored, multi-textured household brooms in a variety of designs. We both stood in silence, looking not merely at brooms, but at a pivotal moment in the making.

"So, how many brooms have you bought, Mom?" I continued to look at the brooms, considering each one and dissecting the possibilities. *Which broom would I choose? Would it be the right one? What type of broom did I want? Would it fit my new place? Would I like the new broom?* My mind raced with the panoply of choices—so many choices.

She stood in front of the brooms as well; straight as an arrow, lost in contemplation.

After a few moments of silence, she spoke. "I couldn't say, sweetie. But each broom meant a new chapter—a different part of my life. Some people just have more chapters than others, and I guess that's okay. Some are harder and some are easier, but I think each one is meant to be a part of your story." She looked at me and held my hand. "So, you just go ahead and choose a broom; it will be exactly what you need right now. And don't ever be afraid to get too many brooms, my girl. Life will take you many places, but don't be afraid. There will always be enough brooms to go around." Her eyes peered into mine. Lovingly, she held my hand until I was ready to make my decision.

I stood silently, taking in her words. I deemed the broom metaphor a welcome gift of knowledge from my mother. I appreciated that she had shared it with me. Regardless of the struggles and traumas she had endured, she was continuously resurging from them. She may not have overcome them with grace, nor did she always move on to a better circumstance, but man, did she ever *try. That's worth something in my book.*

That day, I saw her in a whole new light. She had shown me a place within herself that I had never witnessed. I fancied that she was onto something, and at that precise moment, I decided to just take the leap and let whatever would happen, happen. Heck, I could always choose a new broom.

I reached for the teal blue with white polka dots. An instant smile of satisfaction overcame my face. We looked at each other and approved.

"I think this one is going to do just fine," I exhaled the heaviness.

"Now let's go get you some bedding and some clothes." She smiled at me. We walked through the store holding hands and chatting like old friends. This had been exactly what we needed to reconnect. Things had been strained since I had gone back to school, and I knew she was battling some of her own things. Despite all that, at this moment, we didn't have a care in the world. We went about our business like two seemingly 'normal' women—a mother and a daughter, bonding and having a good time.

CHAPTER 7

The crystallized snow shimmered against our headlights as we made our way through the naturally created, winter-wonderland tunnel of trees outlining the lane that led us home.

What had started as an unbearable day had ended up being a day full of surprises and alleviating revelations. Feelings of contentment and some sort of semblance of pride in myself surprisingly surfaced within me.

There was another vehicle parked beside ours as we pulled into the driveway. I looked at my mom. "Who's here?" I questioned.

She simply smiled. "Come on, lets go in."

The house was lively with music and chatter coming from the living room. Everyone always gathered around the fireplace; it was sacred space.

I recognized the laughter as soon as I heard it—Chelsea and Kyle had come up to visit.

"Hey, dudes!" I shouted. "What the heck? Why are you here?" I hugged them both in turn. Kyle lifted me off the ground as he hugged me tightly.

"Well, I haven't been allowed to play with you all year, since you-know-why," he winked at me. "So, I was thrilled when your mother texted last night and said we needed to come out for some drinks and a good time with my girl."

I playfully slapped him on the shoulder. Then, I looked at my mother quizzically. "Mom, did you do this?" I asked, moved by the gesture—she was full of surprises.

She shrugged in a nonchalant manner and smiled, then went into the kitchen to retrieve five bottles of Coors Light. She came back and handed each one of us a beer. "I think Sophie has a big announcement to make. Come on now, Sophie. Would you like to share with your best friends what's happening?" she coaxed.

It took me a minute to register that she was asking me to declare our newest unfolding. I stood in front of them, ready to proclaim my independence.

"I'm leaving Elijah and I'm gonna move out. It's official. I am currently back on the market." I raised my bottle in the air and everyone followed. The bottles clinked loudly as they all collided with one another and we all shouted a passionate *CHEERS*.

I looked around the room at the faces of the people that truly cared for me. *I belonged*; a beautiful realization that for once, I wasn't alone. I had help. They had not only thrown the buoy for me, they had swam out into the temperamental sea to bring me back. I hoped I would remember this moment when times became challenging again.

"Who wants to hear the new mix I just got in?" Malcolm asked happily. "This is the new stuff. No clubs out here have these mixed tracks yet."

He put on the new compilations and we all danced in the living room. My mother and Malcolm even joined in. I hadn't anticipated becoming a reason for festivities, but it seemed I had. After we danced, we sat around the fire, methodically working out elaborate plans for the next few weeks, leading up to what my friends and family had decided to term Sophie's Resurrection Day.

***

"So, I have an announcement to make," I taunted, purposefully stretching out the pause.

"Go ahead, I'm listening." Paul said, patiently awaiting the disclosure.

"I've come up with a plan to leave Elijah. I'm gonna go through with it once the semester is over," I revealed as I breathed through the anxiety that lingered beneath the surface. "I have help from my mother and my friends, and we have all discussed that it would be best if I simply moved out when he's visiting his parents." I waited hopefully, internally eager to get his approval on the matter.

Even though Paul professionally never really gave his opinion, I really wanted him to commend me and tell me I was doing the right thing. It was one thing to have my mother's biased opinions and my friends' loyal support, but they weren't always the best in judgment, nor did any of them have a great track record of being totally rational when it came to touchy topics. We *all* had issues. So, Paul was my point of reference for normalcy; a beacon to guide me.

"Well, that certainly is big news, Sophie." He nodded slightly, a gesture similar to that of a bobble-head on a dashboard. His eyes squinted as he processed the thoughts crossing his mind.

"Well, what do you think about it?" I asked anxiously.

"Is this something you feel emotionally and mentally prepared to follow through with?" he asked earnestly.

I immediately jumped on the freak-out wagon. "I definitely have to do this. You know how badly I want to be done. I'm starting to realize that I have a sensitive state of mental health, and I need to give myself a fighting chance. I'm not cut out to be in a relationship with anyone right now, Paul." It's not like I never knew I had issues, it's more like I had lived in denial; focusing more on how people perceived me, what I thought were "normal" things to do, and what my mother was up to.

"Sophie, brrreeeaaaattthhhhhe," Paul instructed me through a deep, slow, soothing exhale. "I'm not questioning your reasons. I am asking if you are ready to follow through with this. I'm asking because I want YOU to succeed. I want YOU to have a plan and a support system as you go through with this next step. It's my understanding—correct me if I'm wrong—that your exchanges with Elijah can become *intense*." He looked quizzically at me.

"You're right, they can," I agreed.

"So, please tell me more about this plan."

"Well, the semester is already done, we have a few exams, and then it will be holidays. I've been tolerating our relationship for the time being. Chels and I have already found me a new apartment. It's in the ghetto, but it'll do for the remainder of the year. I only signed a six-month lease there anyway, so . . ." I took a deep breath. "And I told my current landlord that Elijah would be taking over the lease as sole tenant as of the new year. She didn't oppose, so I'm set." Talking about the whole plan intelligibly appeased my anxiety. I was immovable.

"Well, then. Well done, Sophie Ann. You seem to have done your homework. Very good." He smiled. I internally jumped for joy. The little girl in me was saying, *hurray, hurray!* The adult me returned a dull smile.

"Good, would you care to share how the meeting with your doctor went?" Paul asked.

"It went well. He agreed to reduce my medication intake; it may take a while, he said. So right now, I'm sticking to the dosage plan and we will readjust as needed until I'm weaned off." I hated waiting, but the doctor had forewarned me that this was what we needed to do.

"Well, that sounds very good. How have you been feeling with the decreased dosage?" he asked.

"I think I feel fine. I mean, it's been an emotional time, but I'm also trying to convince myself that I'm basically starting over from scratch and that I have to readjust to *feeling* things. You know?" I wanted confirmation, that yes, indeed, this was going to be a process.

"Yes, it is about adapting to the sensations, and also to the emotions you have been dulled to feeling.

So, it would be understandable if you find yourself feeling overwhelmed at times, maybe even feeling depressed again. It is important that you monitor yourself so that you don't fall off a precipice into darkness due to an abrupt alteration of the chemical balance in your brain." He nodded, looking very pensive.

"I'm going to give you some information on what to expect, and hopefully you will be alert to any sudden feelings that may be negative or unexpected." He handed me some information sheets about weaning off of antidepressants. I took them lightly, feeling as though I already knew what to expect, seeing as I had already been down this road once before.

"Thanks, Doc, I appreciate it," I smiled.

"I will be seeing you after the holidays this time. So, I hope that you have a great break, and I look forward to seeing you in the new year." He smiled and stood up, prepared to end the session.

"For sure. Same for you. Happy holidays," I smiled, astounded that the session was already over. It had been such a light and easy session. I hadn't shed one single tear. *Look at me go.*

***

Dusk came early this time of year. I walked out of the office and was greeted by thick sugar

snow falling. The sight was so beautiful that I was compelled to take a walk. As I peered down the street, the fluffy flakes swayed in pure synchronicity.

My mind began to wonder how *it* would really go. Would I successfully *escape*? Or would he somehow show up while we were moving me out? The thought alone unsettled my previous assurance that I had a golden plan—undeniably a genius plan that should not falter . . . not when I needed it to succeed.

I calmed myself down by telling myself that if anything were to happen, at least I knew the scene would be contained and that he would surrender. Maybe all I needed was my mother to be there when I broke things off to make it clear that I was through . . . *have your mommy hold your hand because you're a fuckin' coward* . . . I knew without a doubt that I would not fail; mother had always found a way to execute an escape. She was a tenacious, deliberate woman, and this was not the first time she had preconceived a plan to sneak me out…

***

I was sound asleep when the commotion woke me. At first, I thought the rumbling I was hearing was a train racing across the boulevard, but the sound continued to fester and soon got louder. I sat up in my bed, and that's when I heard his deep growl summon my mother. I heard her footsteps race across the concrete floor. She shouted at him with fierce intensity.

"You can't come in here, you motherfucker! Get out!" her voice shrilled.

I stood against the side of my wall, my body leaning up against it as closely as could be. I poked my head out to see what was happening. I knew better than to make myself visible. My heart was thumping wildly in my chest, but my concern for what was happening far outweighed my instinct to hide. I leaned over a little further to see what was going on, and that's when I was met with the sight of Lucifer crawling through the broken kitchen window like the hellish creature he was. His body hanging over the small window frame resembled a scene from a horror movie.

"I'm coming for you," his demonic voice taunted. "Come out, come out, wherever you are." He sluggishly fell onto the shattered glass spread across the floor, his body sprawled out.

My mother appeared from the hallway that led to my brother's room. There was no sight of Beau. I panicked.

Where was he? Where had he gone? Why had he left me here alone?

"Mommy, Mommy!" I cried. "I'm scared." My childish body shivered.

She rushed toward me and ushered me back into the furthest, darkest corner of my room.

"Where's Beau?" I asked, petrified.

"Ssshhhhhh!" she hushed. "Sweetie," she whispered, "you're going to stay hidden here until I tell you to come out. Do you understand?" There was a marked urgency to her voice.

I nodded my head and held back the whimpering that tried to escape my throat. I swallowed hard. She gave me a kiss, placed a blanket over the top of me, and left me there. I sat tucked against the wall in a fetal position, trying to restrain myself from any movement at all. I could hear her bare feet against the concrete walking toward him, meeting his heavy boots.

"You piece of shit. You thought you could throw me away in jail and I wouldn't come for you?" he hissed vehemently.

His first strike shuddered the house like a violent clap of thunder in the timid summer months. The echo stretched for what seemed like an eternity.

She whimpered slightly. I could hear the scuffle of their bodies moving around the apartment, crashing into all that obstructed their paths. I wished I could move, but my body sat paralyzed. I had promised that I would stay hidden.

"This time I'm gonna kill you, you fuckin' bitch. Then I'm gonna fucking kill those worthless piece of shit kids of yours," he tormented her.

He knew that his words would get under her skin, and that she would fight back. He sought pleasure in her torment; seeing her vulnerability amused him. *We were her kryptonite.*

She shouted inaudible things. Her words came out as gurgles, and then there were loud thuds that resonated across the floor all the way to where I sat. He bashed her body against the living room wall as he choked her. I peeked out from behind the blanket and saw her body pinned up against the wall in my direct line of sight. My eyes rested on her gray, lifeless, bloodied face.

I screamed. The sound tremored from the deepest part of my body. The intense pressure of panic that shot through me was overwhelming. I trembled with fear. My scream had done nothing to loosen his grip on her. His back stayed turned to me; he was intent on finishing what he had started. I knew then that he was going to kill her. I sat in place, frozen in terror.

All of a sudden, the door smashed open and three women I did not recognize emerged from the night like raging warriors. They rapidly tackled Lucifer off my mom. As his hands released her throat, she instantaneously collapsed to the ground as a lifeless corpse.

The third woman was searching throughout the apartment for something. I remained hidden, holding my knees to my chest. I wanted to be invisible. I did not understand what was happening. I was so frightened.

The woman finally reached my room—she had spotted me. She grabbed the blanket off of me and swaddled me into her arms. She knew my name. "Its going to be okay, Sophie, I'm going to take care of you," she whispered close to my face.

As she carried me out of the apartment, I looked over her shoulder to my mother's sprawled, bare feet. I then began to cry…

***

I hadn't noticed that tears were freely falling down my cheeks. I wiped them with the sides of my gloves. I placed my hands deep down into my pockets, shrugged my shoulders up as close to my ears as possible, and walked until the tip of my nose got so cold I could no longer feel it. Once this became intolerable, I retraced my steps back to the parking lot.

"So much for an easy session and no tears," I sniffled.

***

"Hey baby, how was your time away?" He approached me and took me into his arms. I stood there motionless, revolted and annoyed by the contact of our bodies.

He looked at me with pleading eyes. "Listen, baby. I had time to think about what happened the other day. And, well . . . I want you to know that it got outta hand and I'm sorry, okay?"

I didn't need to reply—he had already assumed his short apology would suffice to reconcile our differences. Why would he assume otherwise? It had always been enough in the past. I should have reciprocated an apology too but I remained silent, unpacking the box of food my mother had packed for me.

Elijah leaned against the cupboards, purposefully placing himself in my way—invading my personal space so I would have to speak to him. I knew his tactics quite well, and they annoyed the shit out of me.

"Can you PLEASE step out of the kitchen so I can put my stuff away?" I stared at him, clearly irked. My tone left nothing to the imagination.

"Whoa, what's your deal?" he asked, taken aback by my shortness. "I thought your *little time away* would snap you out of that bitch mood you've had since week three. Why can't you ever be happy, Sophie?!" he complained.

I sighed obnoxiously. He hadn't budged.

"Elijah, I'm trying to put this away so it doesn't spoil. Its been in my car all day . . . now move. And why don't you go make yourself useful and clean up your shit, or maybe even go sweep? Its fuckin' dirty, and that's not from me." I was so done with him. I couldn't even conceal my disdain any longer.

Come on, only a few more days, Sophie.

I shut my eyes, took a deep breath, and released it as slowly as I could. Paul had suggested I try this technique when I was beginning to sense my anger surfacing. *Breathe, breathe, breathe.*

"Jesus Christ, maybe you need a little loving to snap you out of that nasty mood." He approached me and grabbed my ass. "Huh, baby? What do you think?" He bit his lower lip, evidently dismissing my entire body language, not to mention my bitchy replies. For a man who proclaimed his elevated intelligence, he sure wasn't getting it. He still thought that this was all a joke, and that I was . . . what? Playing hard to get?

Oh, how clearly it came crashing into my face—to him, I was merely an object, a dysfunctional object that was not to be taken seriously. *How could you have thought otherwise, Sophie?*

"No, I don't want a good *fucking!*" I snapped back.

How could I blame him? I had allowed others—men, in particular—to treat me this way; just like I had watched my mother allow others to treat her in the same manner.

"What's wrong with you? Can you just fuckin' help around here so I can get this shit done and go to bed, so I can pass my exams tomorrow?" I shouted. Then, I turned my back to him.

"Fuck you too, then." He stepped away and walked the six steps it took to get to our coffee table. He then sat on the futon, clicked on the TV, and rolled himself a cigarette, dismissing all the things I had asked him to do.

"*What a dick*," I mumbled to myself.

***

"Only a few more days until holidays!" Chelsea squealed, skipping beside me like an overjoyed school girl, her grin stretching from ear to ear. By looking at her, you would swear she was the one experiencing something extraordinary.

"Yay." I was not overly enthused by the looming endeavor I had somehow been coerced to follow through with. There was no turning back at this point, unless I wanted to face everlasting disappointment from my mother—I certainly didn't want that.

"Why so glum, chum?" Chels asked. "You should totally be stoked that after the new year, you will have fully regained your independence as a woman, and you'll have a new-found freedom that will invigorate you to the core of your being." She walked backward so that she could converse with me face-to-face. "And I'll get my clubbing buddy back!" She clapped her hands.

"Ya, I know, I know. I just want someone else to do all this, and then I'll happily teleport my sorry ass into the future where all is fine and dandy," I lamented.

"Come on, Soph, you have to snap out of it and see that this is what NEEDS to happen. I really can't stand seeing you so morose anymore." She seemed repulsed. "You've barely cracked a genuine smile all damn year. You do see it now, right?"

She was becoming anxious by my lack of excitement for what was to come. I really didn't want her to think that I was so far gone she had to worry about me. I never had to hide much from her, but I knew I was afraid of what was next. The thought of moving away and finding myself all alone was unnerving. How would I react to my own self, once everyone was gone? *You're a fuckin' baby lala Sophie, suck it up.*

During my entire existence, I always felt alone, *but* . . . I had never really been alone physically for long. I always lived with someone, whether it was a family member or roommates or a boyfriend. The thought of actually being on my own just seemed more daunting at this point in my life, given my fragility and the overwhelming amount of outside stimuli I hadn't had to experience while I was on my full dosage of meds. I was so accustomed to having my every emotion numbed.

In my own defense, normal emotions could drive even a mentally healthy woman crazy.

I was starting to question my rationality and my actual capability to adapt to healthy brain function without my meds. Or maybe I was so fuckin' loopy *because* of my meds? *Hmm, that was plausible reason.* Maybe all I needed was to come off of them sooner. That was something I could come back to later. Right now wasn't the time.

The thought of the Little Engine That Could popped into my head. *I know I can, I know I can, I know I can . . .*

"You are totally right Chels, I feel you. I am so sick and tired of being so dull. So, lets do this final exam and then tonight we go celebrate like its no one's business." I shook my shoulders in dancing motion. "Cuz we gonna *PARTY!*"

I hyped my demeanor because I didn't feel like going in circles about how I was feeling when there was no use in trying to get people to understand. I didn't want her to see how fragile I was. People only care for the allotted amount of time they have decided one should spend wallowing in their own shit. If it lasts too long, people don't wanna care about the same old shit you've been dealing with. They're already over it, so you should be over it, too.

"That's my girl!" Chelsea teased, pleased at my comeback. I deeply wanted her excitement to transpire into my being. I smiled at her.

You can always fake it, I thought to myself.

***

"I'm gonna be getting ready at Chelsea's tonight." I said to Elijah through the reflection of the mirror as I put on my mascara. "We want to go out and celebrate the end of the semester, so you're more then welcome to go hang out with your buddies at that bar you like. Chels and I are gonna head to the club." I made light of our plans, aware that if I made him more interested in hanging with his buddies, then I would be let off the hook.

"I don't know. Why don't we just all go together?" he questioned.

"Because, you're gonna have way more fun with the guys if I'm not around, and worse comes to worst, you boys can always come over to the club." I cajoled.

"Ya, okay. Well, I'll give them a call."

"Awesome, well, I'll see you later." I left without kissing him.

***

The club was packed so full that the people looked like jelly beans inside a guessing jar. The students celebrated the end of the semester with intense eagerness—they were finally liberated from the pressures that had been building all year. The energy was rebellious with freedom. People danced with such fervor they could have been dancing to the beats of a ritualistic ceremony, cleansing themselves of goodness and welcoming evil temptations to possess them. Liquor bottles were popped open as though they were champagne; people stood on the counters pouring directly into open mouths, awaiting the surge of intoxication to envelope us all.

Chelsea and I pushed our way to the counter where a chick was pouring some liquor. We eagerly opened our mouths and awaited the freedom to come our way.

The booze flowed down my chin and in between my breasts, wetting my blouse. Chels and I looked at each other, laughing. The adrenaline rushed through our bodies, excitement and rebellion screaming to be let out. I succumbed to my urge to let my *Girl, Interrupted* loose and let her have some fun.

I jumped up onto the bar, reached over the counter, and grabbed a bottle. I poured freely into my mouth and began dancing with the bartender. The surface of the counter was slick; it made my heels glide until I nearly slipped. The bartender caught me in her arms. The crowd was shouting for a show. People whistled and hollered. I aimed to please, as usual, so I grabbed the bartender by the waist and pulled her into me. *If they wanted a show, I'd give them one.*

I titled her chin up with the bottom of the bottle and poured the liquor into her mouth and down her chin. I looked at her sensually, kissed her chin, and licked her neck, lapping up all the alcohol that had pooled between her voluptuous breasts. I aspirated loudly. I lingered for a moment before I stopped. The crowd was going crazy. The adrenaline was intoxicating. I poured myself a shot and kissed her. Then I turned around and waved the liquor bottle in the air. Everyone was shouting.

"This shit is crazy! Let's get ready to party!" the DJ shouted on the mic.

I danced my way across the counter, pouring shots for everyone standing against it until I made it to the end. I jumped down and got lost in the wave of bodies and hands that emerged from everywhere.

"Holy shit, dude!" Chelsea screamed when I drifted over to her. "Way to let loose!" She pushed me playfully. "All-or-Nothing Sophie has come out to play, and I'm so fuckin' happy to see her!"

She was ecstatic about my doppelganger personality. This was the personality that everyone always enjoyed. The Sophie that pleased, the Sophie that seemed carefree, the Sophie that could accomplish anything and move mountains. She was the Sophie I wished I really was, but for tonight, I was going to let her out and party myself into oblivion.

"My Sophie Ann." Kyle grabbed me in his arms and attempted to bust a move. His gait was awkward on a regular basis and putting him on a dance floor was no exception. He made us laugh. "How you doing?" he said in his best *Joey* impersonation.

"I'm doing so good right now." I continued to dance. The alcohol had overrun my senses and I no longer gave two shits about anything.

"I'm super-happy to see you so light. Its been a long time." He looked at me and I was touched by the genuine, earnest care in his eyes.

"Why, thank ya, buddy." I tapped him on the shoulder and laughed. "Let's just have fun for tonight, all right?" I shouted above the crowd and music.

In the middle of a smoky cloud produced by a combination of the fog machine, cigarette smoke, and multiple sweating bodies grazing against each other, I was safely surrounded by my two best friends. And as it was when we were all together, I knew that we would have one heck of a night, as they had come to safeguard me.

I got lost in my drunkenness. By the end of the night—or should I say by the early hours of the morning—I had walked back home, not knowing who had walked with me or when exactly I had left the bar. I vaguely recall stumbling into my apartment and collapsing on my bed.

Someone mumbled to me, "Sophie, here's the garbage if you need it."

I squinted with one eye open, but I was still unable to make out who it was. After seeing that I was okay, the person left.

Finally, I was alone in my apartment. I lay flat on my back on my bed. The room began to move, so to stop the room from spinning, I dropped one foot on the ground in hopes it would cease; it was a little trick my mother had taught me. She also taught me to eat mustard toast on white bread the day after a hangover (which I would be doing in the morning); that was a trick she had learned from her mother.

***

I stood in my bachelor pad for what would be the last time. The boxes scattered throughout the place made it look that much smaller. I heard my mother coming back up the metal staircase; it vibrated into the sunroom. She came to rest on the other side of the doorframe which separated the sunroom and the main living quarters.

"I'm gonna miss this place," I said.

"I know you are, sweetie," she replied.

I recalled the day I had found this place. I was living in the dormitory with three other roommates at the time. Before I got there, everyone always told me how amazing it was to live in Rez—*you're never alone and you'll make friends*, my mother had said. That year, I thought to myself that it could be the year I got to transform myself into whoever I wanted to be. I could be the friendly, cool girl everyone would love. But once again, who was I fooling?

It was excruciatingly difficult for me to live with these three girls. They all got along, but when I was there, I couldn't get myself to *fit* in—I was suffocating in Rez.

Then, I found the perfect nook, hidden above an old Victorian home not far from the campus. It was perfect. It was going to be *my fresh start*. I was over-the-moon thrilled. The day I moved into that place, my mother surprised me with my first pieces of art;

two floral paintings. One of them said: *Courage is the soul of virtue*—a motto I tried to understand and incorporate into my life.

I found out later that she had been saving up for those paintings ever since she noticed me looking at them every time I visited her at work, until one day they vanished.

After I got the place, it took Elijah less than two months to move in. I never had the chance to commence my Restructuring of Sophie.

How many times had I attempted to become someone different—how many times had I fallen short? This time it would be different . . .

Tears began to flow down my cheeks. I stood there, silently letting them come in hopes they would retreat quickly. I wasn't sure why I was crying, but I knew that this was an ending that would mean something significant for my life, and that down the road, maybe one day, I would understand. For now, my heart ached; sorrow swelled my throat as I leaned against that door. My mother stood by me and wrapped her arms around my shoulders.

"Its going to be okay, Sophie. I promise you that." She kissed my forehead. Then, she gathered two other boxes and made her way down to the truck she had borrowed.

As soon as she left the apartment, my cousin appeared. I hadn't expected him to be here at all. I rarely saw him, but for some reason, we had a deep, unspoken connection—one that many didn't get. He was known as the delinquent of the family; he always had his hands in some sort of illegal shenanigans, but I never cared. I loved him dearly and I think we each could see the sorrow the other hid deeply, and the effort it took to cover it up with all our flaws.

He saw me crying, but he didn't need to say anything. He took me in his arms and hugged me tightly. The gesture released a heavy sadness that had been resting over my heart. I stood in his embrace while it lasted.

I wiped my nose on my sleeve—very ladylike, of course. He tapped my shoulder with his hand, then without a word, grabbed some boxes and started emptying what was left in my apartment.

With all the help, it took us no more than a few hours to empty the place. I stood in the sunroom one last time, staring out at the frozen river. I thanked it for being a beautiful presence; one which had soothed my restlessness so many times before.

CHAPTER 8

The snow was falling steadily as the rays made their way through the morning skies. I stood at the bay window with my cup of coffee, looking out at the picturesque beauty right in front of me. Everything seemed surreal, as though this scene had been taken from a classic black and white picture and placed in this very moment by the keen eye of a scenic designer.

I took in the solitude that encased my being with great difficulty. It had been less than a week since I moved into the new apartment, but I had yet to spend a night there alone. My mother hadn't questioned my avoidance of the place; she either knew the underlying truth or she had gobbled my excuses. With Christmas celebrations upon us, I was able to summon the perfect excuses not to face the solitude I was terrified of meeting. I had escaped Up North, once again knowing I would have other things to keep my mind occupied. One of those things would most certainly be my mother.

"Morning, sweetie." My mother gave me a kiss on the temple. "Merry Christmas," she smiled sweetly.

"Hey, Merry Christmas, Mom." I replied. "It already smells so good in here. Were you up all night basting the turkey?"

"I only got up once. I put it inside a brown bag, so it'll cook nice and juicy. It's gonna be delicious." She placed her fingers up to her mouth and kissed them. Her excitement about preparing our meals always made her gleam. Cooking was her way of saying *I love you*—she knew she was good at it and that everyone would be pleased. She could not fail this; *that* she knew with certainty. Because of that certainty, she was confident that at least the meal part of Christmas would be a success.

We were hosting the festivities this year. It was the first time Malcolm's family and my mothers' family would be joining. By my mother's family, I mean the only sister she liked to spend time with and her kids. We also had invited her cousin, who I also called my cousin. It was certain to be a mismatch of dynamics and the thought alone made me tighten up—I hoped it would go smoothly.

Malcolm's family had always shown a slight disdain toward my mother, which often caused some strife when they were all drinking. Alcohol wasn't always the culprit, though. My mother's tongue often got her into troublesome situations. Malcolm's family showed great affection toward me, but because of their tension with my mother, I was never capable of reciprocating the sentiment due to my loyalty to her.

If they couldn't love her, then I wouldn't let them love me, either.

"Need any help right now?" I asked.

"I would love a coffee, Soph. I'm just going to grab all the good cutlery and make sure it's clean," she said while looking through the knock-off china cabinet cupboards.

"You feeling good about tonight?" I assessed the terrain, checking for any subtle signs that could clue me into which mood she would be in tonight.

"I'm feeling fine. It'll be what it'll be, right? I'm happy as long as you're here, sweetie." She looked at me in an endearing manner.

"Ah, jeez, thanks, Ma," I teased, but her upbeat and joyful persona was starting to become a little off-putting. She wasn't typically the overly-positive, upbeat person. She had been acting this way for a while, and I had come to figure out that she was trying to protect me from something. It was either about my breakup with Elijah—she hadn't mentioned his name *at all* since the decision to move had been made—or she was hiding something. She was pretty darn good at omitting certain details or events to alter or downplay situations.

"You sure, Mom? Where the heck has Malcolm been? I haven't seen much of him at all." I realized he hadn't been around and immediately began to worry.

"He's been helping his parents renovate their bathroom in the basement," she replied, avoiding my stare.

"Really? All day, every day, huh?" I was skeptical.

"Sweetie, its FINE. There it is, now I got it." She pulled out the splendid cutlery set which was used only on rare occasions such as these. She'd found the set a few years ago and had cherished it ever since. She stood up and replaced a strand of hair back into the elastic that was holding it in place. "Okay, I wanted to give you your gift while it was just the two of us." She took her coffee cup from my hands and walked into the living room.

Nestled under our ornately decorated white and blue Christmas tree were three four-by-four pieces of lumber, wrapped with a red ribbon. I looked at them quizzically.

"Umm, thanks, Mom. But what *is it?*"

She laughed at my perplexed look. "Its lumber, sweetie." She laughed again as she stated the obvious.

"I'm glad you find this entertaining, and I know its lumber, but I really have no clue . . ."

"It's a project. I thought we could make it together for your new place." She looked excited. My mother loved little projects. I tried hard to see what she was trying to convey to me, but I lacked the imagination.

"Remember when we had those beautiful wooden candle displays at the store?" she prompted.

"Ya . . ."

"Well, this is going to be *that* when we're done," she smiled.

"Oh ya, I see it now. Awesome, Mom. Thank you so much."

She had a knack for seeing what something could become. I was touched by her consideration, and the fact that she always tried to find a way to get us nice things without paying the huge price. She had so many skills; if only she had some self-confidence, she probably could have made something of herself instead of working at the local Rona, hidden in the tool department.

“I brought out the hole saw and a few cans of stain for you to choose from, so we can easily get this done this weekend, when everyone is gone. You’ll see, we’re gonna make your new place nice.” She squeezed my hand in hers.

“I look forward to it, Mom.” I hugged her tightly. She smiled and went back to the kitchen. I understood, by that remark, that she knew I was avoiding my new place.

“I’m gonna get dressed and I’ll be back down to help you out, Ma,” I shouted from the stairs.

***

I went into my room and grabbed my clothes. On the floor beside the bed, my phone was vibrating. I didn’t have to pick it up to know it was Elijah calling me. Ten missed calls, it said. He was hanging up and redialing incessantly. I hadn’t spoken to him since I moved. I hadn’t even told him I was gonna move, but we got into that fight before I did, during which I told him I was through. He just never heard me and always assumed I was bluffing. Seeing his name on my phone made my heart sink. I didn’t want to deal with him, but I knew that he was unraveling now and that my avoidance of him just ignited an insatiable determination. I listened to the three voicemails he’d left. I was happy I had only paid for the three-voicemail plan and not the ten.

“Sophie, baby. Come on. Answer the phone.” His voice was sweet. I deleted the message.

"Sophie, come on. You can't just leave me like that with no explanation. I deserve an answer. Call me back." His voice began to show his irritation.

I listened to third message.

"Sophie, you're being a selfish ass. Answer my fuckin' calls. I will drive down to your mothers' house and we can talk it through. You can't just leave like that without owing me an explanation. This is my life too. Call me back."

He was trying to unravel me—to scare me into doing what he wanted me to do. He was threatening to come out here. I didn't want to cede to his demands—I was done with him—but the mind games made me uneasy. Maybe I should just do what he wanted so I could get him to back off. Maybe, just maybe, he was right and I *was* a selfish asshole.

I sat on the edge of my bed contemplating my choices. What choice did I have, after all? All I wanted was to be done, move on, and be forgotten, but it seemed that I owed more than I was willing to give. I didn't give a shit if I had to run around this entire country to avoid any more of these confrontations; I would if I had to . . .

My heart raced as I made the decision to ignore his demands.

I sat on the edge of my bed, regaining the little composure I had left inside. It was getting harder and harder to maintain. I exhaled heavily, tilting my head back to prevent the tears from escaping. My mother had taught me that: *hold your head back when you feel the tears coming and it will stop them from falling, sweetie,* she once said to me. I swallowed hard and forced myself to suck it up. This was nothing; I was stupid to let it get to me.

Right now, I had something else to do, and it didn't involve self-loathing. I went downstairs to join my mother in the kitchen.

***

"A little early for wine, don't you think?" I inquired.

She was preparing the deviled eggs for tonight in her pajamas, all the while holding a glass of white wine in one hand and piping the eggs with the other.

"So what? It's Christmas. I can do what I want," she tested.

"All right, fair enough," I relinquished. There was no point in attempting to make her see that regardless of the specifics of this day, it was still only ten-thirty a.m. Maybe even on Christmas this was a little early?

"You can have a glass, too," she offered.

"No, Mom. Thanks, but I'll have some *breakfast* first. Would you like some?" I hoped she would tune into my accentuation of the word *breakfast.*

"No way, I'll be eating a big meal later and you know I don't eat when I cook," she answered.

No, it's because you fill your stomach with booze that you don't eat, I thought to myself. I obviously didn't say this out loud. She would have profusely denied such accusations.

"Are you sticking around today?" she asked.

"I'm just going to help you out here today. I don't want you slaving away all by yourself. Usually it's just you and I doing this. And if I'm not mistaken, you always make the same amount of food!" I laughed. So did she. She *always* made huge batches of food. You'd swear we were a family of ten, not two.

I took a bite of my peanut butter toast. I chewed and chewed, trying to force it down. The lump in my throat was still there, blocking my natural urge to feed myself. The pasty residue lingered in my mouth, so I grabbed the wine glass from my mother's hand to chase it down. *Fuck it, I might as well indulge, too. It's ten-forty-five a.m., and like good ol' Alan Jackson would say, it's five o'clock somewhere, right?*

***

The house smelled like Christmas should: chicken and dumplings, stuffing, ham, a whole turkey, mashed potatoes, gravy, cranberry sauce, and of course, veggies galore. The table was lit with the incandescent glow of white and red candles. The kitchen lights were dimmed to summon an ambiance of sophistication and elegance that was abnormal to our typical Christmases. Our dinning room looked like a page out of the *Chatelaine* Christmas edition.

"Wow, Mom. We did *all this.*" I said as I looked at the masterpiece with sheer amazement. This is what life in a "normal" house on holidays probably looked like. I felt a pang of resentment, and also one of pure satisfaction.

She smiled with pride—*or,* maybe it was the twinkle of a buzz? Maybe a little of both. Oh well, it was Christmas, after all. This was a time of celebration and indulgence. For today, we could have it all.

The frigid winter breeze shot through the kitchen as the door swung open.

"Oh my god!" shrieked my aunt. "Look at this place." She stomped her snowy boots on the mat.

The open door continued to let in the cold winter air like a swift, invigorating burst of liveliness. The rest of the crowd soon followed: aunt, uncle, cousins, boyfriends, and the in-laws came stumbling in through the cold Christmas night, all at the same time.

"Jesus, did you guys all carpool?" I laughed.

"Merry Christmas, y'all," everyone said to one another, exchanging kisses and hugs. Giant, beautifully wrapped boxes and bags were exchanged between hands until Malcolm and I trekked them to the living room and placed them around the tree.

As we gathered around the elongated dinner table, chatter flowed freely throughout the house. Laughter sprang from the depths of our bellies and was expelled loudly. Cutlery clanked against plates and the popping sound of corks ejected from their bottles resounded all around. The spirit of Christmas had overtaken the house for the first time.

After dinner was done, we all proceeded into the living room, where the space had been cleared of the furniture that usually encumbered the fireplace. The large space that remained had been set up as the perfect dance floor. Malcolm did the honors. Wearing his Santa hat, he passed out the gifts one at a time until none remained under the tree. I went upstairs and retrieved one last one—for my mother.

"Here, Mom. This one is from me." I handed her a small box. Inside was a delicate, white gold, heart-shaped pendant.

“Its beautiful, Sophie. You really shouldn’t have. Thank you so much.” She teared up and embraced me tightly.

“I’m glad you like it, Mom.” I fastened the chain around her delicate neck. The tiny diamonds glittered as the light danced off of them.

As the last gift was opened, Malcolm cranked up the music and grabbed my mother in his arms. She clung to him with one arm laced around his neck. Their foreheads rested against one another as they closed their eyes and shared a love which had no barriers. My aunt and uncle joined in, and so did Malcolm’s parents. The sight was mesmerizing. I leaned against the wall, drinking a strawberry daiquiri my cousin and I had made, taking in the unusual and oh-so-wonderful displays of affection. My heart was light with content and . . . *joy*?

Mom seemed happy-drunk, and for once, the two families were flowing easily in the same space.

“Oh no, Sophie!” I heard my cousin scream my name. I rushed to the kitchen.

“Holy shit!” I burst into laughter. Red strawberry puree was splattered all over the counter and the cupboards. “What the heck are you doing?” I asked in between gasps of laughter.

My cousin stood bent over laughing at the mess she had made. “I tried to make another batch of daiquiris, but I forgot to put the lid on,” she said with tears flowing down her cheeks. The laughter boomed from her chest.

I pulled two straws out of the drawer and handed one to her.

“No use in wasting,” I told her. “Drink up!”

We both stood over the mess with our straws and begun to drink up the splattered daiquiris.

After the laughter had subsided and the booze had enacted its effects on everyone, my cousin leaned into me and slurred, "Your mom isn't so bad tonight."

Well, maybe its because everyone is at the same level, I thought to myself.

"Ya, she's been doing really good," I said protectively. I didn't want to jinx or put attention onto her drinking tonight. There had been no scenes thus far, and I had prayed like a little girl to the heavens repeatedly for the day to go smoothly.

"Well that's nice to see," she said. "We don't want to repeat what happened last year..." she trailed off.

Ya, last year...

***

Last year, my mother and I went to celebrate Christmas at my aunt's house. As per usual, my mother began grumbling about how we *had to be on our best behavior.* By *we*, she meant *her*. She always included me into her soliloquies while she attempted to plan every move of the evening. Although she forcibly denied her alcoholism, she knew when it would be tough for her to reel it in. One of those times was in front of her sister, whose judging eyes and pointed jabs seemed to unsettle her, sometimes to the point of unraveling that which we tried to keep contained.

So, of course, under the "pressure of performance," my mother yielded to the thing she had tried full-heartedly to avoid. She got wasted. She began slurring attacks on her sister, including questioning my uncle's motives as to why and how he could be married to her sister. The list of insults went on and on, and I knew that she would feel bad about it all in the morning. After several of us shed tears, I was finally able to coax her into going to bed.

It was no different that year than many others; those Christmases were no different in that they were all challenging—she hated Christmas for a reason I still do not know. Above everything else, I had to suffer through the pitiful stares she seemed to ignore.

Then, I overheard my cousin's boyfriend whisper:

"*How embarrassing is your drunk of an aunt? Wow, it's a good thing your family isn't like that. No wonder she does nothing good with her life, look at her.*"

I paused when I stumbled upon the whispers. The tears swelled my eyes before I could consciously process what exactly had been said. A lump formed in my throat, and my fierce, protective nature overcame me. The anger and sense of betrayal I felt toward my cousin, and her "who does he think he is/shit don't stink" boyfriend soured my sentiments toward them immediately. From that day on, I had an understanding that they had always seen, and would always see, us as *inferior*.

***

I took a sip of my drink and found a seat beside the window. I tried to make out the silhouettes in the distance, forcing my brain to switch tracks from the summoned recollection.

The music had dimmed down to a light background hum, and almost everyone had spread out to find a place to sleep. I was lost in thought when she sat beside me.

"How are you, sweetie?" she slurred. Even under the influence, she always had a knack to *see me.* That gesture, and that part of her being, was the reason I forgave her over and over again for *everything—every time*.

"I'm okay, Mom. How are you?" I scrutinized her.

"I'm okay too," she said as she took a sip of her beer.

"It was a pretty great Christmas, hey?" I asked.

"Ya, it was," she agreed. Then, she was silent for a moment. As she lit her cigarette, she swayed. "The only thing missing was your brother." She took a long drag.

I didn't have to look at her to know that she was crying. She usually cried when she talked about him.

"Ya, I know," I replied, feeling the pang.

"I wish he would just come home. I wish he would stop hating me. It hurts so bad, Sophie." She held onto her cigarette like a lifeline, inhaling deeply as if to suppress the incoming surge.

"He doesn't hate you, Mom." I tried to soothe her. "He's just stubborn and hurt. He doesn't hate you." I hugged her.

"What if I die, Sophie, without ever getting to hold my son again? Doesn't he know that he only has one mother? That I did my best? But I love him. And I'm so sorry," she cried.

I kissed her salty cheeks. "You're not dying anytime soon, Mom. He'll come around one day, when he's ready." I said this with certainty out loud, but deep down, I only hoped what I spoke was true.

I cannot recall how many times I've made up stories about my brother to comfort my mother. There are too many to recount, but most of them happened when she knew I would see him at school, when the pain of him leaving was still fresh . . .

"Ya, he says he loves you. And he hopes you're doing good," I lied one day, as I did on many days prior and afterward. My fourteen-year-old self wanted to appease her sorrows, which were so ripe at the time.

What really happened was I would run into my brother in the hallway at school and chastise him for not calling Mom, and for avoiding me. I would call him a selfish asshole, and he would usually tell me to shut up. My heart would twist in my chest. Then, I could feel my obligation overrun my feelings, so I would lie. I had lied to her about him since the day he ran away to our dad's when he was twelve years old.

To this day, it remained the same.

Somewhere along the way, she must have forgotten that I was still her child. I wasn't my brother, but I counted—at least I thought I should. I remained loyal to her. I loved her. I was the one that became her confidante; her reliable other half. Had her longing to have her son back diminished the worth I held? Or maybe she *did* silently blame me for his running away? Had she forgotten about the child she wrote notes for, the notes she tucked into her paper lunch bag almost every day? Why couldn't I just be enough? At times, all these questions hurt as much as the twisted look of agony that resided on her face when she spoke of him. Would I ever be loved as much? And why did it feel like even though I was a constant in her life, I would never add up to the significance of him?

She sniffled and took a swig of her beer to chase the dryness in her throat. I did the same.

"How about we get some sleep, Mom? I'm pretty tired," I said, once again always trying to coax her.

"You go ahead sweetie. I'm going to clean up a little before."

I didn't protest. I knew she would get it done.

"Night, Mom. I love you." I kissed her three times—on the left cheek, the forehead, and the right cheek. She closed her eyes tightly, allowing only one tear to escape. I hugged her, lingering there for a moment. Then I went upstairs, leaving her in the shadows of the night

CHAPTER 9

"What the fuck did you do?" he shouted at me, ignoring the crowds that walked by.

I tried to maneuver around him, but his body blocked me each way. So, I stopped and looked him dead in the eye.

"Listen, Elijah. I told you we were done. I wasn't kidding. So fuck off." I looked up at him and saw the panic and anger that swirled in his stare. My heart raced with anticipation for what was to come. He wasn't happy.

"You just fuckin left me. Like that. And you think I don't get a say in all of this?" he asked.

"No, actually you don't get a say in all of this. All of this," I gestured to myself, "does not belong to you. Am I clear? It's over." I stepped aside.

The people who passed us in the hallway deviated out of our path as would a shoal of fish.

"You're a selfish bitch, Sophie. After everything that I put up with, for you!" His pain was visible.

I swallowed hard and avoided looking at him. I resumed walking in the opposite direction, hoping he would get the message and not create a bigger scene.

"We'll talk about this later, Sophie!" he shouted.

I knew he meant it.

At that moment, Kyle walked past me. He spun around and jogged to my side.

"What's up, Soph?" he asked, looking worried. My clammy, pale skin had alarmed him.

"I just ran into Elijah," I said. "I think I'm gonna puke." My heart thumped in my chest. My stomach tightened, and I suddenly became light-headed.

"Breathe, Soph, it's okay. It's okay," Kyle repeated. He wrapped his arm around my shoulder as we walked.

"He's pissed and hurt. He's not just gonna back off," I told him.

"I'll walk you to your classes, and I'll make sure that I'm waiting for you when you're done, okay? Don't worry," he tried to console me, but his attempt fell short. I knew better than to doubt Elijah's capabilities and determination to get an answer that he was content with. Our breakup hadn't been his choice, so I wasn't going to get off the hook so easily.

"Thanks Kyle. I appreciate it," I replied. *I'm fucked.*

***

As promised, Kyle was at my classroom door waiting for me when I was done. The sight of him eased the tightness in my chest a little.

"How was class?" he asked.

"It was all right. I'm just super happy that I'm out of the school for the next few weeks with my practicum. I won't be seeing Elijah around, and I really need to stay away from him while things cool down."

"That's awesome. A breather will give you time for the dust to settle and before you know it, both of you will be on your way to forgetting the other even existed," Kyle said, sounding hopeful.

We had just received our new assignments, and thankfully, the remainder of the year would mostly be completed outside of the classroom at our chosen placement. I had decided to return to the same practicum facility I had previously attended. The juvenile institution offered me as much comfort as it did the clients who went there. Nobody would dare say they enjoyed it, but honestly, the rigid structure of our daily tasks offered all of us who suffered from instability in our lives a much-needed relief from the chaos. Besides, I was already familiar with the place, and I wouldn't have been capable of handling a new environment.

Before the beginning of the holidays, I had abruptly ceased my meds—against recommended orders, of course, but I was sick and tired of waiting around for it to be done. I felt like I could handle pretty much anything, and with my frequent visits to see Paul, I'd never felt more capable of handling myself. The anguish from the move had settled and given me a new-found, fearless determination to get this year done. I was certain I had this shit figured out.

Walking with Kyle away from the classroom, I could feel my fragile foundation trembling under the pressure of normal function. Maybe I had quit too fast? I wasn't sure if the fact that Elijah had shaken me up was the culprit behind the weird thoughts and feelings I was beginning to sense, or if they had always been there, muffled and subdued by the antidepressants.

Maybe I should talk to Paul about this next time I see him.

***

"You've been doing a remarkable job here with us, Sophie." Walter said.

"Thanks. I really enjoy working in this program. It definitely has its challenges, but every day is different and the structure remains the same. I like that," I replied.

"Well, you have an evaluation coming up in a few weeks. Seeing as you've been with us for a while, you know the programming. So, I'm going to ask that you facilitate some of the programs on your own." He paused, then continued. "Now, I know that may seem daunting, but don't be intimidated by all this. You already know the program and the clients here. I wouldn't allow you to go through with it if I didn't think you could handle it. You're a natural, Sophie," he praised.

Walter placed his large hand on my shoulder while he spoke. He gave me an approving smile and rubbed my back, lingering his hand for a brief moment.

Then, he left me to look over the program files. He walked out into the unit, leaving me alone in the office with the security guard.

"That's a pretty big step, Sophie. I must agree with Walter. You're doing real good here. You fit right in," the security guard said. He had been sitting silently in the corner of the office, looking at the monitors that displayed every inch of the unit.

"Thanks Grant." I smiled back at him; taking the compliment with great difficulty.

I placed my shoulders straighter and inhaled deeply to remove the tension I felt. My mentor—the one who was teaching me all the tricks of the trade, all the secrets to becoming a great intervention worker—had quirks of his own, to say the least.

He had displayed signs that were all-too-familiar to me—displays of alcoholism lit up like Las Vegas all over him. No one ever seemed to see it, or bothered, so I never spoke about it. Of course, self-doubt and uncertainty as to what I was observing stopped me from addressing it; *maybe I was projecting?*

Walter's close buddies worked for the same organization. If something were really off about him, I would think they would have addressed the issue—interventions were the name of the game here. However, that didn't change the fact that I was training to *be* observant; to see subtleties that could be alarming or potential threats. Something was definitely off.

Regardless, none of that changed the fact that he had been doing this job for a very long time, and he was really good at it, too. He was an ol' timer with decades of experience who I had the opportunity to learn from. He was kind and thorough in his teaching methods, and very insightful; this was invaluable know-how that I was going to absorb as much as possible. Alcoholic or not, I had been assigned to him, and I wasn't about to let a minor setback in personal choices dictate my success rate. I had an alcoholic mother, after all. Walter knew about her, along with other details of my upbringing which had come out during certain conversations. I had a lifetime of experience with alcoholics, and I wasn't going to treat him any differently.

Apparently, functioning alcoholics were a more frequent occurrence than I had once thought.

***

I sat under the dim light of the lamp filling out the clients' evening notes after they had all gone to bed. The only people who remained were Grant and me.

I could see him through the glass window of the office, making his rounds throughout the unit, investigating to see that everything was as it should be. Although he had the stature of a giant man, he moved around with incredible lightness.

"Hey, I was wondering if you'd like to go out for a drink?" he suddenly asked, pointing his flashlight at me.

"Who? Me?" I replied, trying to block the glimmer of his light with my notebook.

"Ya, you. A bunch of us usually go out for a drink at a little tavern not far from here. I think you should come, you know, seeing as you're practically one of us now," he said, smiling.

"Umm, ya. I can do that," I said hesitantly. I hadn't been around any of my coworkers outside of work. I didn't even know if it was frowned upon by my department at school. I hadn't read anything anywhere about it being some sort of misconduct, but I didn't know for sure. Anxiety surfaced, causing a hundred questions to unravel in my mind.

He noticed my perplexed expression. "You don't have to say yes. Its an open invitation, that's all." He sat down and swiveled his chair in circles.

"You're just like the kids," I laughed, throwing a pencil at him.

Grant was easygoing, and one of the favorite security guards we had around. His humor was what he typically used to de-escalate tense situations. His all-around nice guy attitude always made everyone smile.

He stuck his tongue out at me in a childish way just to prove that I was right.

"Ya, I'll go. It'll be fun," I said, smiling.

So, we waited together for the night shift to come on. I followed his lead through the town until we pulled up at the old, raggedy tavern. Grant gallantly held the door.

"Hey guys, look who I brought?" he announced, pulling a chair out for me.

Around the table were three other coworkers and my mentor. Everyone greeted me with polite ease.

"I hope its okay? I wasn't sure if I was allowed to come out for a drink or not?" I asked openly to everyone, but pointed my stare at my mentor. Walter leaned over his glass, grabbed the pitcher of beer, and poured me glass until it overflowed.

"There's no problem at all, dear Sophie," he slurred.

"Of course not," the others pitched in.

They all resumed talking about work and projects, adding in a few comments about unfavorable clients who they tried to pawn off on one another. I found myself immersed in the conversations, feeling like this time, I was a real part of a team. I belonged. They had taken me in, officially, as one of their own—like birds sweeping me under their wings and showing me the real world. I laughed all the while, soaking in every moment of this privilege I had been granted.

Things were looking up.

"So, how are you finding it, really? No need to filter right now, were all just friends," one of my coworkers asked.

"I really love it. I feel like it's part of me, like I was always meant to be doing something in the likes of this," I answered.

"You certainly conduct yourself like a natural, and we're all really pleased with your drive. None of us can say that we are disappointed, or that our shift is gonna be tougher with you on. You pull your weight, and in this job that's a big deal," one of them answered.

"Well, thanks. I appreciate the feedback." I felt a swell of pride expand within me. The sensation of doing something right was exactly what I needed. A sort of respite had shown itself, and I fully clung to it as though I were begging for it to grant me clemency against my repressed inner-unraveling.

Slowly, they all left. The only ones remaining at the table were Grant, Walter, and myself. Walter swayed against the table as he pushed himself to a stand.

"I'm off to bed, kids," he stammered. He fumbled with his pockets.

"What are you looking for?" I asked.

"My keys, I can't seem to find them." He tapped his jacket pockets, then his pants pockets. Incapable of finding them, he seemed perplexed as to where they could be.

"Well, it's not a big deal, Walter," Grant piped in. "There's a cab outside waiting for you and I'll pick you up tomorrow for work. We work the same shift, so no worries, man, Sophie and I will find your keys for you," he offered.

"I guess that's all right, good night then." Walter stumbled out the door.

"See you in a few hours, man," Grant called after him.

Once he was gone, Grant dangled the keys in front of me.

"You took his keys?" I asked.

"Ya, you've probably heard the rumors, and well, they're true. The guy's an alcoholic. It's not the first time he would have driven home drunk. I just can't let him do that while I'm around, so I took them."

He said this with such kindness; such sincerity with no want for praise. I looked at him with pure awe and realized that he was what he showed everyone: an honest, genuine, kind man. I think he was the first man I ever encountered who really didn't have a hidden agenda or something that he asked for in return. He was the first man I sat next to who allowed me to completely relax. I sat there reeling in these thoughts through and through, amazed at what I was experiencing. I had never been around such an exceptional, selfless being.

"Sophie, are you okay?" he asked, looking at me with an intrigued expression.

"Oh, ya," I snapped out of my daze. "Sorry, I was on the moon." I smiled.

He laughed. "Well, thank you for joining us tonight. It was nice getting to know you outside of work." He looked into my eyes, his stare stirring a whirlwind in my stomach. "Maybe we can do this again?" He paused and patiently waited for my response.

I licked my dried lips; my throat felt parched. How was it that I had never noticed him before today? My relationship with Elijah and my personal issues had stripped me of outside awareness. I had been surviving for so long that this moment felt like the first time I had ever come up for air since I could recall—if ever. I could have easily soaked up all the time I possibly could in his company. His funny, calming demeanor crumbled my walls without effort. Just in those few hours I spent with him, I felt like he had lifted the veil. I was frazzled.

"Um, Grant . . . I just broke up with my boyfriend. It's been rough. I want to give myself a chance, and if I start going out with you, then I'm just gonna lose myself in you. I can't do that right now, no matter how amazing you are." I felt a pinch as I spoke. What was wrong with me? I had a great man in front of me asking to spend time with him and I decided to say no to *him*? I was all sorts of messed up.

"I'm sorry to hear about your break-up. As I recall, though, it didn't seem like a great relationship. I overheard you a few times talking to him on the phone. I didn't mean to eavesdrop, but it's kinda my job." he said easily. "I'm not asking you to marry me, Sophie, I'm just saying that if you ever want to hang out again, well, the invitation is and will always be an open one. No pressure, okay?" He stood up; I followed suit.

The sky sparkled with billions of illuminated stars that seemed more brilliant in the country winter night air. The full moon glistened against the snow. We stood beside my car, our breaths intertwining, dancing in the frigid air. I was thankful for the refreshing burst of air; our conversation had ignited a fire within me that I thought could never be kindled.

"Thank you for taking me in as part of the team," I finally said. "And, Grant? Thanks for your kindness. Its weird; I'm not used to men like you, but I like it." I smiled. I could get used to this.

He chuckled. "Anytime, Miss Sophie."

He hugged me and we went our separate ways.

CHAPTER 10

The ringing of my cell phone woke me with a startle. I clumsily searched for it, knocking everything off my nightstand. Finally, I found it underneath my binders. *Who would be calling me at seven-thirty in the morning?*

"Hello?" I answered groggily.

"Hey, Sophie. Its Malcolm."

"Malcolm, hey. What's going on?" I was instantly alert.

"I'm sorry, I hope I'm not waking you, but I had to call you before I went in to work this morning." He sounded hesitant.

"Ok . . ." I replied.

"I wanted to be the first to tell you, because I don't want you to wonder what's going on." He took a deep breath. "Your mother and I are separating, Soph." He paused.

"What do you mean? Why?" I sat up straight in my bed. My heart throbbed. This couldn't be happening—not right now.

"I can't do it anymore, Soph. I am so sorry. Your mother is getting out of hand. She's always angry and moody with everyone. I can't bring her to any of my events or to family gatherings because you know how she can get. She's drinking *so much* that it's eating half our paychecks."

I could hear the struggle in his voice. I ached for him and for us. She needed him. *We* needed him. What was going to happen now? My mind began to swirl.

"So, what's gonna happen now?" I asked.

"I'm moving in with my parents until your mother can find a new place to live. I'm not kicking her out—I want her to take the time she needs to find somewhere she will be happy with." He paused again. "I love her very much, Sophie, and I love you, too. This doesn't mean that you and I have to stop talking or seeing each other. You are a daughter to me, you know that, right?" he questioned.

I remained silent on the other end, swallowing and registering what had been thrown my way—what all the implications from here on out could be. *How am I going to manage now? Lord, I need saving.*

"I know, Malcolm," I mumbled. I understood the burden he had tried to carry for all these years. I had hoped profusely that they would finally get married, but it had never happened. My childish mind thought that marriage would have guaranteed that he wouldn't escape; that he would have to try that extra mile before giving up. Malcolm, however, had already raked up enough miles with my mother to never have to put up with anybody else's shit *ever again*.

The tears flowed down my cheeks as he and I silently held onto the line, as though this were our last-ditch effort to remain unchanged, as though we could undo what had been done, but it was lost—and forever would it remain broken.

"I'm sorry again, Soph, but I will see you around town when you come Up North, okay?"

I avoided a reply to that question. I knew that he was trying to make it better. I also knew, that eventually, I wouldn't be seeing any more of him.

It would be my loss too.

"How's Mother taking it?" I asked.

"She's taking it as well as she can, I guess. You know she never really shows me her real feelings, so she's pretty pissed. You should go down this weekend so she's not left to her own devices. I know you have so much on your plate, Sophie. I tried. I really tried," he pleaded.

"All right. Well, thanks for telling me, I guess." I cleared my throat. "I'm going to miss you, Malcolm," I admitted.

"Me too, Sophie. Me too. Listen, I'm always here for you, no matter what. You finish your schooling and make something amazing of yourself, do you understand? You deserve a great life, Sophie Ann. A great life. So don't mess it up because of her. We all love her, but she needs to fix herself. Take care. I love you."

He waited for my reply, but I remained mute. After a minute he said *okay*, and the line went dead.

I listened to the dial tone, unaware that I hadn't hung up yet. The continuous hum mingled with my unraveling mind. I was stumbling over what I needed to do. *What* would I do? I lay back down in my bed, staring lifelessly at the ceiling. I wondered what the tipping point had been. Was it the years of her abusing his love and kindness? The drinking? The foul mouth? The unfixable, perpetual sadness? He certainly deserved happiness and a woman who appreciated the wonderful man he actually was. Even after so many years with her, he had remained energetic and happy—albeit tired and resentful at times, but never for long. He *had* tried; that I knew, but something deep inside me couldn't help but hate him for abandoning *me.* During all those years, he had allowed me some respite from the burden of her. For nearly five years, I had someone to tag in, so I could finally be away long enough and begin to focus on the possibilities of a different life. He had given me enough time to breathe . . . and now he was gone.

Once again, as the story always repeated itself, I was left alone with *her.*

My head ached. I got out of bed and grabbed some pills to alleviate the pain. I swallowed hard. I had to put my shit aside and see for myself how she was handling it. I dreaded the impending, recurring downfall I knew would follow suit. I'd deal with *me* somewhere along the way. For now, *she* needed me.

***

"Ma!" I shouted as I entered the house. I looked around. Nothing seemed different to the naked eye, but of course, I knew better. She had to be home; her car was parked out front and I knew she hadn't been into work a few days. Malcolm had told me.

"Mom, where are you?" I dropped my bag at the front door and wandered around. The house looked immaculate and there wasn't a noise to be heard. I walked upstairs and found her lying in her bed, sound asleep. The smell of alcohol lingered in her bedroom and beside her bed stood an empty bottle of white wine. I knew she was sleeping off her hangover. I could have banged pots and pans together and she wouldn't have flinched an eyelid.

I leaned against the doorframe and watched her in her slumber, as I had done many times before. The insurmountable sadness, pity, and betrayal suddenly invaded me. It was useless to wake her—she wouldn't be coherent enough to answer the questions that caused me so much anxiety. I decided to leave and come back later. I'd go pay a friend a visit instead.

***

"Hey Julien," I said with a *surprise!* expression when he opened the door.

The look on his face was one of consternation more than one of delight. "Hey Sophie, what brings you here?" he asked, holding the door semi-open.

"I just thought I'd come and say hey. Aren't you gonna let me in?" I coaxed.

He opened the door wide and gestured for me to come in. "Of course, sorry. I'm just so surprised to see you, that's all." He followed me to the living room. "After all that crazy shit with your boyfriend—" he began.

"Ex boyfriend—may I be precise on that fact right now," I interrupted.

"Oh, really? Well good for you. That guy was something else, man." Julien's entire demeanor suddenly changed into a more relaxed state. "Well, I hope that your presence here won't get me in trouble, will it?" He looked at me with slight annoyance and concern.

"Jeez, of course not. Relax. I'm here because I need a distraction." *Who am I trying to fool? I'm the one that needs to relax.* I collapsed onto Julien's couch, startling his giant orange cat. "Oh, sorry little man." I grabbed the cat and cuddled him onto my lap.

"So, what's really going on, Sophie?" he asked as he brought me a tall glass of red wine.

I knew Julien still held much of the endearment toward me that he had when we first began to hang out. Our "relationship" was one of sporadic get-togethers, spontaneous declarations of love, and vows that he would take care of me if only I would stay with him.

I, on the other hand, knew I would eventually fall short of his expectations of the type of woman he thought I was. To crumble his idealization of what and who he thought I was seemed more crushing to me than the actuality of telling him I was incapable of love. I didn't know *how* to love. I wouldn't have met his expectations, nor those of his wealthy family, *I would never fit in with them.* Who was I but merely the daughter of a poor drunk, disowned by her father, left alone to her devices to stumble through this maze called life. He deserved so much better than me. I figured that in reality, I was doing him a favor by not reciprocating his endearments. So, finally, we agreed to a no-strings-attached engagement—it suited us.

I took a huge gulp. "I'm here because my mother needs help with something. I won't be staying in town long and I *really* needed a distraction." I raised my eyebrows, diverting the subject and trying to convey my desires without exposing my fragility all at the same time.

"Oh, I see," he said, getting the point. He smiled at me and moved across the room to where I was sitting. He lounged his arm behind my back and leaned in for a kiss, a big, elaborate smile displayed on his face. *This wasn't our first booty call.* I kissed him back with great eagerness. I yearned for a feeling greater than the internal torment of my being. I needed someone to help fill the void of nothingness I held inside.

I sat there reciprocating the intense exchange of tongue and mouth. Hands and limbs sprawled over one another in a feverish frenzy of intense desire. His was a desire of want and excitement. Mine was a need for survival; a way to grip myself into my body and try to shock it into anything but the numb, sucking, energy-drinking vessel that I carried around.

I surrendered to him as we made our way to his bedroom. I lay fully bare and exposed—fully at his mercy. Yearning, repenting for my indiscretions—for my existence. Needing, wanting to live, all the while feeling my soul cascading into the abyss of never-ending turmoil.

I lay on my back with my eyes tightly closed while he made love to my body. The tears cascaded town my checks as I allowed myself to shatter with every stroke. And when it was over, I shuddered with pure disdain for the person I was.

"Are you okay, Sophie?" he asked, looking alarmed. "Did I hurt you?" His face contorted with concern.

I stood up and gathered my clothes. "Of course not, Julien, you've been nothing but a welcoming gentleman. Don't worry, I'm just a tad off right now, that's all." I turned my back to him and made my way to the washroom.

I stared at the reflection of the woman that looked back at me. She was still a vessel of nothingness. Nothing had changed. I returned my stare with one of anger and disappointment. *How could someone who had lived through hell be so weak?* I scolded. I took a deep breath and clothed myself. Determined, I refused to allow this frail reflection to show her face again until I dealt with what needed to be dealt with.

"Thanks so much for everything, Julien," I said with my jacket flung over my arm. "I'll see ya around, okay?" I kissed him on the cheek.

He was accustomed to my ways. He took no offense, and I believe that's why it had always been so easy for me to come and go as I pleased with him.

He smiled and pecked me on the cheek. "Soph, if you need anything at all, you know I'm here for you, right?" he said endearingly.

"Of course," I said as I walked out of his house for the last time.

***

She was in her usual spot in front of the fireplace when I came back. The country station was blaring on the television and the fireplace was roaring with intense heat. I hadn't told her of my unannounced visit; I rarely made my way home during the week.

She looked startled when she saw me arrive beside her. I bent down and gave her a kiss on the check.

"Hey Mom," I said, stepping back to get a better perspective.

"Oh my god, Sophie. You scared the shit outta me!" she shrieked. "What the hell are you doing here?"

"I just thought I'd come for a visit, that's all. I have two days off right now to complete some practicum assignments," I said matter-of-factly. "How are you doing, Mom?" I looked her square in the eyes and shot her *her own* famous stare. She seemed taken aback by my assertiveness.

"Well, I'm as good as I'll ever be, sweetie. Why?" she asked sourly.

"Well, Mom, because I know. That's why." I took a seat beside her and pulled out my pack of smokes. I took two out, then lit one for her and one for myself.

"Thanks," she mumbled. Suddenly the façade ceded way to her true disposition—sadness.

"Well, are you gonna tell me what happened? Or, are we just gonna sit here like nothing happened at all?" I asked forcefully.

She sat silently, dragging her cigarette to mid-point. She exhaled the smoke halfway and took a giant swig of her beer. I sat there waiting for her to come around; for her to finally admit that she had fucked up once again, and that we were in a bind.

Finally, she said it.

"Malcolm left. He's moved back with his parents," she said with great scorn.

"Why, Mom, why did Malcolm leave?" I pushed.

She flicked her cigarette into the fireplace and lit another, handing me one too. I refused it. "Because he's a coward who couldn't handle the truth about his family. That's why," she spat. "That's why, sweetie."

She looked at me with great confidence in the words she spoke. If any other person had been sitting beside her, they may have believed the outrageous allegations she claimed about my now-ex-stepfather. Unfortunately, at that moment, her daughter was the recipient of the false claims and inaccurate recollections as to why things had gone this way. Her confidence in her twisted assertions made me bite my lip. How could she still lie to me when she knew I knew? Did she really live so deep within her world of sickness that she believed her lies and her deceits as truths?

I squirmed uneasily in my seat, wanting to shout at her and all the while wanting to hug her and tell her that we were gonna make this work—this was what we did, we made things work. “Fuck, Mom. This is just really fuckin’ shitty and I really hope that this isn’t actually the end,” I said instead. *God, please make me right!*

“Sweetie, don’t worry. I’ll be fine.” She took another swig of her beer, emptying it and placing it on the ground with the other corpses she had accumulated. She then got up and made a run to the kitchen for more, coming back with four beers for her and me. I had no energy nor desire to protest the offerings. I took the beers with a great sense of relief, knowing I would ease up just a tad to make it through the rest of the night.

The house looked the same, but it had changed. It had lost a pivotal mechanism that had made it something great. *We* had lost Malcolm, and the void his absence created was much greater than the naked eye could see. I sat there thinking of how I would go about this. Would I stay here and help her get her shit together? Or, would I leave her to her own devices and hope for the best?

I couldn't stand to see her go back to those shitty basement apartments; over my dead body. The thought of them alone sucked the sheer life right out of me. I was certain I would find a proper solution eventually. For now, I wanted her to hang tight for a little while; to gather her composure so we could create a methodical approach to this turn of events.

Function, Sophie, function.

"Stay here for a while, okay? Don't go moving your shit out into one of those nasty places, okay Mom?" I pleaded.

"Okay," she replied simply. For once I think she was too exhausted to put up a fight. Maybe she finally realized she had done it; she had gone and screwed up something great and there was no way of undoing what had been done. I knew Malcolm was gone for good. The thought made me nauseous. Looking at her with her beer resting upon her raised knee, I wondered if she felt the same.

I didn't feel like asking.

***

My fatigue was made obvious by the darkened circles under my eyes. I hadn't slept well in months now. I hadn't eaten well, either, and I was functioning on pure vapors. The demands of my practicum had increased. The team felt that I was a considerable asset to their program and had even mentioned the possibility of hiring me immediately after its completion. I wish I could say I was thrilled by the offer, but I couldn't get my brain to recognize the magnitude of the possibilities in front of me.

"Hey you, where's your shine?" Grant asked as I stood motionless, blankly staring at the files in front of me.

"Excuse me?" I asked, confused as to what he was implying.

"You seem off. Is everything all right?" he asked, concerned.

"Umm, ya and no, I guess. I'm going through some stuff right now," I said, snapping out of my daze. I braced myself and summoned the fake charming allure that I had to exhibit while I was surrounded by people. It was suddenly struck by the pure hypocrisy I had been living. I was just like my mother, except she was hiding a disease of addiction and I was hiding the dis-ease of not knowing how to *be*.

Grant walked over and stood beside me. "Hey, Sophie. You want to talk about it?" he asked with a look of concern.

"Um, this isn't the right place for it. I'm gonna go outside for a smoke and I'll be right back. Do you mind watching the clients?" I asked as I grabbed my jacket and access key and headed out the door.

"For sure," he replied.

I stood in the gated yard taking in the fresh air. The chilly morning was a welcoming relief. *Man, am I ever gonna snap out of it?*

No, no. You got this Soph, I encouraged, trying to fool my brain into believing what I was saying. If I could inspire tormented, delinquent kids to have some sort of hope, I sure as shit could at least fool myself into believing in possibilities, right? Paul had told me about my self-sabotage and the fact that I was my own worst enemy. I felt like I needed to fail to be where I belonged, or something along the lines of that. I stood there trying to re-play the conversation we'd previously had.

"Shit," I said aloud. I couldn't even remember the conversation where Paul had told me that. *Dammit, Sophie.* I inhaled and exhaled deeply several times, exaggerating the exhale as to *let it go.* Let what go, exactly? Maybe that was the problem right there. I didn't even know *what* the exact problem was anymore—I was just a whole shit-pile of *shit.*

With perfect timing as usual, as though he had overheard my battered thoughts, Elijah messaged me: *Sophie, I miss you. I'm so sorry about how things went. I just want some closure. Can we talk?*

You've got to be kidding me. I butted out my smoke and made my way back to the unit. I didn't have time to be wallowing. *Snap out of it.*

"Here's my paper on the philosophies of the organization, as well as a revamped version of the morning sessions and why I think we should merge two programs as to target the underlying issue—as observed by me—that clients do not have a toolbox with adequate coping mechanisms. I believe this merge will increase the success of their communication abilities and reduce outbursts and anxiety in the long run." I handed Walter my second-to-last assignment, feeling a subtle decrease in pressure on my shoulders. *Almost done, girl,* I told myself.

"That's wonderful, Sophie, thank you. I'll revise these tonight," he said, skimming my paperwork. "I've said it before, but I'm very pleased with your work here. Keep it up." He winked at me and smiled. I reciprocated a polite version.

"Nice," Grant chirped in from his control center—the pivoting chair—as Walter exited the office. "So, the clients are on study block right now—you wanna share your troubles with me?" He leaned as far back as he could in his chair, interlocking his fingers.

"My mother and stepfather separated, so now I have to find her a place to live," I said without hesitation. There was something magical about this man and his ability to ease my sorrows without even trying. I was comfortable around him.

"I see. But why do *you* have to find her a place?" he asked.

"Well, because I don't want her to end up in a dump. I'd like for her to have a nice place, you know? But she can't really afford anything on her own . . . so I feel like I'm between a rock and a hard place," I admitted, discouraged.

"Hmm, understandable, but that's a lot of pressure you put yourself under. Well, if you ever need anything, here's my personal cell. Call me whenever." He handed me his number. "I know you'll find a solution, you're smart." He got up and walked among the clients, exuding confidence and calm that everyone around him soaked up as though he were the first rays of summer sunshine. Once more, I looked at him in awe. *He was different.*

I saved his number.

The night shift came to relieve me from my duties. It had been a longer shift due to some issues involving two boys and a cut-up can of 7-Up. I shared the shift change with the night guard and left feeling weary.

"Safe travels," Grant piped in as I left the building.

***

The nights were less frigid as the seasons transformed. It was a nice change from the winter driving I had endured all those months along the country back roads. A few intermittent miles of pure darkness and poorly paved roads stood between me and the highway to my apartment in the city. Although I was the first to complain about the drive, I really did enjoy the sights throughout the different seasons. The northern mountains were a rarity with their stunning array of tree species, which made the landscape bloom with all the hues of green one could imagine. In the fall, they would shine with all varieties of mosaic colors, colors that purely displayed the true essence of Mother Nature's palette. During winter, the snow would be strewn with pristine splendor over the mountains and through the valleys, glistening like a brilliant carpet of snowflakes. I also thought how wonderful it would be within the next few weeks, when the first blossoms would give way to a drastic change of scenery. After being dormant all these months, the mountains would erupt with transformation once again. It was quite fascinating.

The light from my phone blinked incessantly, sending a glare into my eyes. I slowed down and checked who was calling. I didn't recognize the number, so I decided to pull over and answer.

"Hello?"

I heard someone clearing their throat. "Hello, Sophie. It's Walter."

His voiced sounded strange. I couldn't quite put my finger on it. "Hey Walter. Is everything all right?"

I asked, slightly concerned. He had never called me on my cell phone before. My heart palpitated in my chest. I couldn't understand why he would call me at midnight unless I had made a major mistake at work. *What did you fuck up this time, Sophie?*

"No, I, umm, was just looking over your paperwork here, and I couldn't help but think how amazing you are," his voice was sluggish.

I figured it out. He was drunk—he was drunk-dialing me.

"Well, thank you, Walter. Is there anything else I can do for you?" I didn't want to appear rude. He was still the dictator of whether or not I passed my practicum.

"I can't stop thinking about you, Sophie. You only have a few weeks left and I can't help but want to make love to you."

As he uttered the words, I felt a violent tremor cross my body.

"Pardon me?" I asked, not believing what I had just heard. *Maybe I misunderstood.*

"I need to make love to you, Sophie. It's something I just can't help. I think you're a beautiful woman. Please," he stammered.

I hadn't misunderstood after all.

"Listen, Walter, I cannot believe what's happening here. I know you don't mean what you're saying right now. I'm gonna hang up now." My voice vibrated with anger. I gritted my teeth so hard I could hear the crunching and taste the debris which had broken off.

"Sophie, wait . . ."

"Get some sleep, Walter. You're drunk." I hung up the phone and threw it on the floor of my car in disgust.

I couldn't understand how someone I had looked up to as a mentor could be capable of such repulsive conduct. I held my stomach and my chest, trying to suppress the urge to vomit—my body's way of attempting to reject the overload of shock it was under. "ARRRGGGGGGGG!" I screamed in agony and betrayal as I pounded my hands on my steering wheel.

I had entrusted him with details about my life that no other person had heard me speak out loud—besides Paul. He knew about my issues with men. He had power and authority over me. He had deceived me into believing he was genuine. It was as though he had committed the act simply by uttering the words. I was disgusted. *Had I indicated in some way that I wanted this?*

My entire world seemed to collapse around me. Why was I being tormented in such a way? I no longer had an escape from the unbearable affliction eating away inside me. Everything was so confusing . . .

Why did life have an incessant determination to obliterate everything I tried to accomplish? Why did men think they could possess me? What gave them the impression that I was nothing more than a worthless object meant to satisfy their desires? Like the man who thought he had a right to place his hand down my pants because I had showed him ten minutes of interest, or the guy who had groped my ass as I walked by, or the one who had used his body to corner me and intimidate me into submission. Or my grandfather, who had used trickery to touch me in ways no child should ever be exposed to...

***

"Mom," I said faintly.

"What's up, Sophie?" she said with her back turned to me; folding laundry on her bed.

I stood in silence, trying to gather the courage to speak. Every time I opened my mouth, the words refused to come out. I swallowed repeatedly, trying to moisten my throat; hoping I could coax my voice to spew the words so I could be done with it. I had tried so hard to hold it inside. I didn't want to ruin things for her—for us.

But I couldn't take the secret anymore. I didn't want to play his games. I didn't want to be tickled. I didn't want to be quiet.

The words finally fumbled out of my mouth.

"I don't want to go say hi to Grandpa anymore," I mumbled, keeping my gaze at my feet while I clenched my hands together. *I was ashamed.*

She stopped what she was doing and turned around to look at me. I was standing in the doorway of her room; her eyes zoomed in on me like a hawk.

"Sophie? Why don't you come here, sweetie, and talk to me?" She took me by the hand and gently walked me over to the bed to sit down with her. "Sweetie, did something happen?" Her voice was slightly pinched with a tinge of knowingness. She didn't need me to say more to know what had happened. She took my little face in her hands, forcing me to look her in the eyes. "Tell me, did Grandpa do something to you?"

I nodded my head *yes.*

She let out a low cry, the shock robbing her of words. She held me in her arms as we cried together.

I never had to go sit by Grandpa again, *nor did we ever talk about it after that.*

***

All these self-entitled men; couldn't they see that I didn't want any of it? Didn't they understand that every time I gave in, it shattered every shred of dignity I had within my soul? Didn't they know that their touch made me feel so worthless that I began to believe the only way I could possibly be loved was to submit to their every whim? What did love mean, anyway?

I had to be a good girl . . .

I cried. I cried for the weight I had borne in my soul since I could recollect. I cried because of the hopelessness I felt. I cried for the person I seemed to project onto the world.

It had to be *my fault*; all of it had to be happening because I was doing something wrong. *Right*?

Please, Lord, please help me. Help me cleanse the filth that has encrusted upon my soul, so I can finally breathe.

I lay with my head against my steering wheel, sobbing in despair. What was I except for the embodiment of everything I despised? The world wanted the best of me, and by this point, it had succeeded in taking it.

After a long while, when my head had ceased spinning, I placed my car in gear and drove full throttle all the way to the city. No policemen nor traffic was anywhere to be found. Of course, when I was looking for trouble, trouble wasn't there. *Fuck.*

CHAPTER 11

I called in sick for the remainder of the week and I never once heard from Walter. I must have showered twenty times in the last few days, too. I couldn't get the sensation of filth off of me. Why did I feel so dirty?

I still had to attend my late classes that week. Thankfully none of them consisted of anything too demanding, and I was actually looking forward to the distraction of my pottery class, *maybe I'd try to smile today*. Although I royally sucked at pottery, I always felt some sort of soothing effect when I played with the clay. It was alluring to have my hands create something from a sheer lump of clay. I also got one heck of a kick out of the professor who taught the class. The poor man evidently believed I had no natural inclination toward the art of pottery and thought all my creations turned out to be either atrocious, too heavy, unfit for use, or possible weapons. While it was true that they may not have been usable, my mother thought I created the most beautiful art, and because she believed that so much, she even had all my pieces displayed in that knock-off china cabinet's glass shelves. No, she hadn't displayed fragile crystals or fancy plates—she had chosen to display her daughter's atrocious art. No matter how many times she faltered, she showed a mother's unconditional love in her own way . . .

It was nearing six o'clock by the time I got out of my course with a bag full of pottery. I walked outside and set out for the furthest parking lot. The lots were bare except for the few vehicles that remained—mine included. As I got closer, I could see that someone had parked behind my car. I paused in my tracks for a minute, trying to decipher who it was and what was happening. I proceeded with caution. As I got closer, I recognized the car; then I saw Elijah step out. My throat tightened. My heart stopped.

I looked all around me to see if I could spot someone else walking, or if any other cars were coming—nothing. *Why did I park so fuckin' far? Of course—because I thought I needed the extra exercise. That'll teach me.*

I tried to avoid eye contact and walk around him, but he placed his body in front of my path, forcing me to halt. "Sophie, listen. I don't want to cause any problems. I just wanna talk, okay?" he pleaded.

"If you don't want to cause problems, Elijah, then why are you even here?" I shouted. My patience and my ability to reel myself back had been shot out the window when Walter crossed the line. I was fed up with being pushed around, with being used. Maybe if

I straight-out acted like an aggressive bitch, maybe then men would finally back off.

"Sophie, come on. Don't be that way, you know I love you." he cooed.

"Elijah, I don't want to talk to you; now move your fuckin' car so I can leave," I said, slightly panicked. I had parked my car up against the soccer field, so my only way to escape was to drive across unless I could get him to move.

I felt trapped.

"I'm not leaving until we talk." He placed his body against my driver's door.

"There's nothing to say. It's over. I moved. You get to keep *my* apartment, everything remains all fuckin' dandy for you, while I had to move all my shit because you couldn't understand two words, *GET OUT*!" I vibrated with anger as I tried to move him out of the way.

"Who are you dating now? I know you wouldn't stay by yourself for long, so who is it?" His cheeks reddened, and I finally understood the scenario he had played out in his head.

"You have gone and lost your mind," I said vehemently. "I'm not dating anyone, not that it's any of your business. I see what this is all about, now fuckin' *MOVE*!" I shouted.

He moved over slightly but tried to hold my door shut. "Why won't you just tell me the truth, Sophie." He stared at me.

I finally gave in and looked at him with tears streaming down my cheeks. I gently held his warm face and peered into his steel blue eyes "Elijah, don't you understand? Don't you understand that I can't love you, I don't want to love you . . . I don't know how," I pleaded. "Please, please, please just leave me alone. We ruin each other, *I'll ruin you.* We don't bring anything good into this relationship. When we are together, things hurt even more for me. I can't stand the hurt any longer, Elijah, please go away. Just leave me alone. If not for me, do it for yourself. Find yourself someone who will actually make you happy, who will love you. Just let me go." My heart ached; my pleading had drained all I had left.

Elijah slowly moved his body in surrender. No matter how much he thought he loved me, I knew he understood that I would never let him. I could see the pain that we had inflicted upon one another. I could see the real source of our anguish. The underlying truth of our painful attempt at love was that we were frightened people. What he was afraid of, I could not say, but I knew that the demons we tried to hide within ourselves would always find their way out. If we stayed together, we would become the source of the others' demise.

I slammed my door shut and put my car in gear. I didn't care what I had to do; I was going to get away from him. *I was going to get away from myself.* My head spun as I clutched down in first gear. I drove across the field, escaping. I looked in my rear-view and saw him get into his car.

I panicked.

As I was about to plan my next move, Elijah turned his car the opposite direction.

I exhaled and dialed Chelsea.

"Chels, its me." I said

"What's up, Soph?" her tone concerned.

"Can I come over?" My voice trembled.

"Ya, for sure babe. What's going on?" she asked.

“Elijah was at my car tonight. I think it’s done for good now.” I sheepishly explained to her what had just happened.

***

She opened her door as I pulled into the driveway. My eyes void of life, I walked into her house without speaking. She closed the door behind us and wrapped her arms around me. She cloaked my invisible wounds with her love. I rested in her embrace and cried.

I was overcome with fatigue.

“Chels, can I go and take a nap. I don’t wanna go home just yet.” I made my way to her room and laid down in her bed.

“Soph?” she asked.

“Ya?” I uttered.

“Are you gonna be okay?” she said, looking perplexed.

“I don’t know” I mumbled through my exhausted eyelids.

***

I woke just as tired as I had been when I laid my head down. I could hear the bass from Chelsea’s music echoing through her house. I pulled myself out of bed and wandered around looking for her.

“Hey girl, how did you sleep?” she smiled as I approached her.

“Not so well, I guess.” I slumped down onto a chair.

“Listen, I hope this shit is truly done between you two,” she said matter-of-factly.

"Umm, I guess" I huffed. "I just don't even wanna think about it. It makes me queasy." I was still unable to grasp why things had been going so haywire lately. It all seemed to be pushing me into a corner where there was no escape—nothing to do except spontaneously implode.

"Listen, go into my closet and grab some clothes, we're going out," Chelsea instructed.

"I don't think I feel like it. It's Thursday and everyone goes out on Thursday," I contested.

"Nope, we're gonna head downtown tonight and stay away from here. Kyle is on his way. So let's get going." She gestured for me to hurry.

I doubted their attempt to console me would be effective. I also knew this *distraction* wouldn't be helpful either. From my vantage point, this felt like a no-return. I was tired. "Fine." I pulled myself off the couch and got ready.

We went downtown looking for fun, but I wasn't in the mood for partying much at all. I wanted to curl up in a ball and stay there until life had decided to leave me alone. With everything that had been happening, it felt like I was a locomotive with a mechanical failure, gaining speed at a frightening rate. I was completely lost and out of touch with the things around me.

The booze went down faster than the next round could arrive. The sting of the liquor burned as it reached my stomach. I welcomed the feeling; I needed it to numb the anguish that had become so cumbersome I could barely move.

Chelsea and Kyle followed suit, pacing themselves. All evening they stood by my side, which was out of character for them. They were like dogs sniffing out dis-ease. Normally I would have enjoyed their company, but tonight I couldn't help but want to scream at everyone to just leave me the fuck alone. Nothing could rectify how I was feeling.

After a short two-hour stay at the club, I was done. The amount of alcohol I could tolerate had already been surpassed after the first time I vomited. The violent explosions propelled the large quantity of fluids out of my body. The putrid scent caused me to vomit some more, until finally, I simply gagged from the lack of substances to expel from my body.

Chelsea stood behind me in the bathroom stall, holding my hair and rubbing my back. "It's okay, Soph. It's okay," she quietly repeated.

I slumped down onto the dirty bathroom floor, listening through the haze of my spinning head to the girls' rambunctious laughter as they stumbled around the bathroom, looking through their bags and fixing their makeup. I couldn't stand the happiness—the lightness of being that all these people so easily exuded. The thought made me angry; it made me sad.

"I want to go home," I mumbled. Mascara ran freely down my clammy cheeks.

"For sure," Chels answered. She placed her arms around my waist and helped me to my feet. We walked together across the bar until we spotted Kyle. Without uttering a word, he placed his arm around my waist and walked me to the car.

"I want to go to my home," I said as I stumbled into the back seat.

I could see them exchanging glances, questioning.

"I want to be alone," I said again. "Please."

"Sure," Chels said.

I passed out in the back seat until the car came to a stop. The short nap had lessened some of the dizziness, but the residual acidic taste of the bile remained, lingering in my mouth. My head had regained some of its clarity after I vomited. Kyle and Chels walked me up to my apartment.

"It's okay guys, you can go now," I ushered them toward the door. "I'm fine."

They both objected at the same time.

"I'll stay here with you," Kyle offered.

"No," I asserted. "I'm tired and I want to sleep. Please guys, just go," I begged.

They finally gave in and left me alone.

I leaned against the door, relief rushing through me. I shuffled my way to the bathroom and bent down to reach the faucets and turn on the bath water. The steam began to fill the small space; within minutes the condensation had claimed the mirror. I wiped it with my sleeve and stared at my hazy reflection. My vision went in and out of focus as I tried to clean the mess of mascara that surrounded my eyes. The effort was futile, but I managed to smear the black residue all over my cheeks. I began to cry, as the person who looked back at me no longer resembled a real human being—she was but the empty carcass of a girl who had tried so hard to become a good woman.

I stripped my clothes off my body, releasing myself of all physical constraints and dropping them to my feet. I entered the steaming bath. The heat encircled my body as would a hot blanket. I lay in the water, allowing myself to submerge until it reached my nostrils.

I rested there as my mind began to whisper and taunt me with thoughts of death. The idea began to permeate through me like the spreading of a wildfire on a windy day.

I surrendered, renouncing all efforts to fight back. And then, as though my body had been mysteriously overrun by an outside force, I stood up, exited the water, and walked to the kitchen. Water puddled around my feet as I sifted oh-so-calmly through the cutlery drawer, knowing exactly what I was looking for: my red-handled paring knife, a gift my aunt had given me when I moved into my last apartment.

I walked placidly back into the bathroom and sat down on the teal-blue bathroom mat. My naked body feeling exposed, I began to tremble.

I hung my head and began to cry. I cried for the insignificance of my existence.

I held the knife in my right hand and mindlessly began a horizontal back-and-forth motion. The sensation, although it stung at first, became numb-surreal. I wept, not wanting to die, but wanting the suffering to end.

The blood began to mesh with the crimson of the handle. Through the blur of my tears, I looked down at the surreal scene before me. As suddenly as I had begun, I stopped in mid-stroke. In disbelief, I took in the mess I had made. I wondered: *who was this woman sitting naked on the bathroom floor, alone and cold?*

I trembled violently as I tried to reach for my phone, my hands stained with the vital fluids that had dripped from my body.

I dialed Kyle. His phone went to voicemail.

"I did something bad. Can you come over?" I cried in panic.

I placed a towel on my wrist to alleviate the bleeding. I wanted it to stop. I lay on my floor, huddling my legs up to my chest as I shivered. Exhaustion had overtaken me; my mind ceded way to the darkness.

I awoke with Kyle shaking me back to life. "Sophie, wake up, wake up!"

I tried to escape the fog that had overtaken me. I blinked, wondering if it had all been a nightmare; maybe my turmoil had only been imagined and I had not done what I thought I had done.

"What the fuck, Sophie?" His eyes bore the look of betrayal and confusion. "What did you do?" He held me in his arms as I began to weep again.

"I don't know. I'm so sorry!" I wailed.

The torment of my weakness had shaken me to my core. Kyle sat with me on the floor, cradling my naked body in his arms as one would a fragile infant. He swayed me back and forth as his tears dripped against my cheek, uniting with those that escaped my eyes.

Kyle lifted my towel to expose the gash. The laceration was not as deep as I had anticipated it would be. It wouldn't need much attention.

I sighed with relief, my heart releasing a powerful ache that had been suffocating it. I thanked the God that must be looking over me.

"Let's clean you up, Soph," he said, uttering the words in a hushed voice.

I nodded. He lifted my weary body off the floor and held me in his embrace. He emptied the bath, allowing the water to drain before he turned on the shower.

As the water rushed out of the shower head, Kyle stripped his clothes off, exposing himself to me. He reached his arms around my waist as he guided me to step into the bathtub.

The water stung with warmth against my skin, thrashing against my battered body. Though the battle had been mostly invisible to the naked eye, my physical being ached with such intensity that I was experiencing the painful aftermath of a horrible accident.

My tears were relentless.

Kyle lathered a facecloth, and I watched the ghost-white bubbles expand as he rubbed the soap against the cloth. I braced myself against him as he proceeded to clean me, with great awareness of the carnage I had endured. He proceeded to wash me with such deliberate care and attention that the love he exhibited for me softened the agony within.

It was in this moment that I had an epiphany: *I wanted to live.*

I wanted to have a good life.

I needed to try harder.

I would try harder.

I looked at him, and finally, some of the haze that had covered my sight lifted.

"Kyle, thank you," I whispered.

"Always, Sophie. Always," he said as tears once again began to rush down his face.

I could feel his heart swelling with pain, and I came to realize that there *was* kindness and love around me. There was no uncertainty about that.

***

The morning light shone through the car window as we drove down the highway. I rested my head against the cold glass, embracing the contrast as I welcomed the heat of the sunshine to warm my face. Chelsea sat in the back seat with me, holding my hand in hers. She held onto my hand during the entire car ride, and didn't let go as we walked together into the waiting area of the doctor's office.

"What do we have here?" The doctor gave me a quick glance as he sifted through my intake form. He was fairly young. "Miss Sophie Ann," he mumbled.

He grabbed my forearm with minimal gentleness and removed the make-shift bandage we had put on. He analyzed the wound as he twisted and bent my wrist.

"Well, this is not that bad of a laceration." He looked at me with disapproving eyes. His judgement stirred the embarrassment I now carried. "Looking for attention, weren't we?" He proceeded to treat my wound. "Next time, you must cut vertically," he said shortly as he placed the Steri-Strips on my wrists.

I swallowed back my tears, knowing he was right—I was screaming for help, not for death. The words stung with poignant truth, but his lack of empathy shook me.

Chelsea gasped. "Are you outta your fuckin' mind?!" she screamed at him. "What is wrong with you? You're supposed to help her, not reprimand her!" Chelsea's voice shook with anger and disdain. I placed my hand on her shoulder.

In less than ten minutes, I was bandaged up and out the door, but I would forever hold the shame that came with the stigma of suicide.

In the weeks that followed, I worked closely with my doctors. Paul and my doctor agreed that the best intervention plan was to resume an adequate dosage of my antidepressants. They both assumed that my abrupt cessation of my meds had caused the unwanted and harsh withdrawal effects—one of them being suicidal thoughts. I hadn't followed through with the initial intervention strategy I had been given, and thus, I had led myself into the perfect storm. My brain couldn't take it, and even though I thought I could handle it, it turns out I wasn't tougher than chemical imbalances.

According to my doctor's regimented plan, it would take me months before I could successfully and safely wean myself off my antidepressants, but that was a plan I was more than willing to abide by.

CHAPTER 12

I walked into the unit with trepidation. It was my first shift since that night everything had come crashing down, and I anticipated there would be an uncomfortable sit-down. Although we hadn't scheduled one, I figured if Walter had any recollection whatsoever about that night, he would want to rectify the situation. The thought made my anxiety flare up, but I had talked this exact scenario through with Paul beforehand. I had chosen to keep the incident hushed for many reasons: fear of repeating the same shame that stemmed from when I was a little girl guided my decision.

I had told my cousins that Grandpa was touching me, their response was: *why would Grandpa do that to you and not to us?* They *didn't believe me*. I feared the same reaction would occur in my current situation, so I preferred to just keep my mouth shut and do what I needed to do at the time: *suck it up.*

Paul thought that facing Walter would help build my confidence and allow me to know how it feels to hold the power of assertion.

I listed the things we had talked about:

- Don't become reactive.
- Listen while he speaks.
- Breathe.
- Respectfully assert yourself that this behavior will not be tolerated.
- Clarify that if anything of that nature occurs again, he will be denounced to his superiors.

The metal door slammed shut behind me, activating my survival mode. The adrenaline rushed through my veins, causing my heart to pulsate with intense vigor. I halted and leaned against the cold, gray door. I closed my eyes and forced myself to inhale deeply: *In through the nose, out through the mouth—count backwards from a hundred until my heart regains its normal pace . . .*

Ninety-nine, ninety-eight, ninety-seven, ninety-six, ninety-five, ninety-four, ninety-three, ninety-two, ninety-one, ninety, eighty-nine, eighty-eight, eighty-seven, eighty-six . . .

I regained my composure. I stood up straight, lifted my chin, and just like that, I was ready to see his face.

Walter looked at me with the eyes of a scolded pup; his demeanor proved to me that he remembered the revolting thing he had said.

I inhaled, preparing myself for the culmination of my practicum. *How would it end?*

"Sophie, I will start by saying I am deeply sorry." He uttered the words with a sentiment of remorse. "My actions were unacceptable, and I know I cannot undo what I have done." He looked at his feet. "We both know you would have passed this practicum without this incident ever occurring, but because of the circumstances, I thought it would be best if I just handed over your final grade and this." He handed me an orange envelope.

I took the envelope and lifted out the contents. The header on the page said: *Letter of Recommendation.*

If it hadn't been for the current situation, I would have been thrilled to receive a free pass to *Go*, so to speak. But at that moment, I couldn't help but hear the voice of self-sabotage trying to peep in. *You're only getting this because he wanted to fuck you.*

Paul had warned me that I needed to be aware of this voice when it came, and that I would have to address its falsehood immediately, so it wouldn't get carried away and bring me down

Shut up, you don't get a say this time, I told the voice.

I cleared my throat. "I have no words to describe the betrayal that has occurred. All I can say is that after this is all over, I will not be applying here. I have already sent in my application to another organization. I cannot stay around here anymore."

I heard myself speak with such composure. The woman speaking didn't sound like me, *but she was.* This was the me I was going to be: confident and capable of asserting myself in a respectable manner just like Paul said I could.

"I am thankful for all that you have taught me, but when these few weeks are over, this will be the end of our relationship. I have no interest in ruining your career, but I do think you may need to address your issues."

My heart was finally relieved of the burden, as though the act of acknowledging the issue and addressing it had automatically alleviated the weight and importance it had carried. I had discovered the magic trick. Was it possible that it was something called forgiveness?

Walter acquiesced without a word and walked out of the office, leaving me alone with two envelopes that officially released me into the world of educated professionals.

I sat down in Grant's swivel chair and gave myself a spin. I tilted my head back and closed my eyes, allowing the twirling sensation to lighten my heart. An unrestrained smile spread across my face; I was free.

"I don't mean to interrupt, but you're in my chair." I could hear the playfulness in his voice.

"Oh, muffin," I said, turning to face him. I gave myself one last swivel before I released the chair back to him.

He laughed and pulled a piece of paper out from his back pocket. "Here, I think this may help."

I looked at the piece of paper. "What is this for?"

"It's the number of a guy that used to work here. He has a house Up North; it may work for you guys."

"Thank you." I held the piece of paper as though it held all the significance in the world; another weight would be lifted if this worked.

"I told him a little about you and your situation. He's expecting your call today." Grant winked at me, as though he were a genie with magical powers.

I walked over to him and gave him a hug. His large arms gathered me in the warmest embrace I had ever experienced. I lingered for a moment, soaking in every single feel-good sensation I was experiencing.

All these feelings were foreign to me. Was this how functional people experienced the world?

No wonder people thought life was good. As I realized in that moment, once you open your eyes to the possibilities, the world rushes in to show you more love and compassion than you could ever know what to do with.

"Thank you," I whispered against Grant's ear.

"Anytime." He released me, his blue eyes locked into mine as though he could see the depths of my soul. I held my breath as though my entire being recognized the pure essence of his gaze.

I could love him.

***

Grant's lead turned out to be fruitful, after all.

"That's the last of it," I said as I dropped the last box that read *kitchen* onto our new butcher counter-top.

Mom and I both stood in the space that would become the kitchen/living room. The abnormally high bar counter stood erect in the middle of both spaces, creating the divide. The house was not nearly as lavish and spacious as the house on the lake, but at least it was a quaint little house in a cul-de-sac. As a bonus, there was a quiet river flowing right across the street.

Mother had been so detached from recent events, so lost in her grief and anger, that she hadn't even noticed that we had not seen each other, and had merely spoken twice, in the last two months. I guess I couldn't have chosen a better time to have a mental breakdown.

I had gone ahead and signed a temporary lease agreement for her and I. We would finally be living under the same roof, only now simply as roommates.

Things had been eerily simple over the last two months since *my incident*. It was as though the world had fallen back and given me a moment of grace.

I had finally graduated and was now waiting for my contract position to begin with the other organization. Things were finally looking up.

"So, what do you think?" I asked. "You've been awfully silent." I looked for a hint of something, *anything*.

She lit a cigarette and leaned against the counter "Its okay, Sophie. I guess it's cute." She dully replied.

I couldn't help but feel a pinch of hurt toward her lack of enthusiasm and recognition for all I had done for her. After all, I had literally fallen apart and glued myself back together piece by piece—*and* found us a new place to live.

"Well, at least you get to live with the best daughter ever," I attempted to coax her out of her sour mood. Even though I detested her melancholy state, I understood that she was heartbroken and needed time. *We both did.* This living together thing would be good for both of us. At least I hoped it would.

"Look what I got us." I took the broom out from behind the door.

She smiled at me.

"I was told by a wise woman once that you always buy a new broom when you move somewhere new." I handed her the new burgundy broom.

"That was a nice gesture, sweetie." She smiled faintly.

"Hey, you know what? Let's go do something crazy," I said.

She raised her eyebrows quizzically.

"Come on, I'm taking you somewhere," I said with a big smile.

"Where are you bringing me, you crazy kid?" She finally grinned. It had been a long time since I had seen her smile.

Success.

We pulled up to the new shop that had opened up in town: Blue Bird Tattoos. She looked at me. "What are we doing here?"

"I've decided that we are gonna get matching tattoos that will symbolize the true love in our lives. What do ya say?" I asked excitedly.

"Well, it looks like I don't have a choice, now do I?" she teased.

We were greeted by the buzzing noise of the tattoo gun and a pretty, redheaded girl that had more piercings and tattoos on her face than I could count. She smiled widely. "How can I help you girls today?"

"We'd love to get some matching tattoos." I looked at my mother.

"Ya, that's right, matching tattoos," she echoed.

"Well, if you're not looking for anything too crazy, Donny will be available within the next ten minutes." She looked at us, awaiting a reply.

"Ya, that's perfect, we'll wait," I said. I looked at mom and shrugged. "Hey, it's gonna be fun."

We waited patiently for Donny to be done. "What can I do for you ladies?" he looked at my mother for an answer as he approached.

"My daughter and I want matching tattoos; how about three stars?" She waited for my reply. I nodded.

"Ya, three stars, that's easy. Where would you like them?" Donny asked.

"On the foot would be nice—I always wanted one there. What do you think, Mom?"

"Ya, I like that idea," she agreed.

"So, who's first?" Donny asked with a smile.

Mom went first. We decided to go with the three stars: two small ones that represented my brother and I, and one larger star that represented my mother. In only ten minutes, she was out of the chair. She never uttered one word or even squinted to say that it pinched.

"Look at you go, not a peep," I teased.

"Want me to hold your hand?" she teased back.

"Very funny." I stuck my tongue out at her as I grabbed her hand.

It was a welcome sight to see some life pop back into her demeanor. I hadn't been too engrossed in my own life to notice that she had lost a lot of weight. I was hoping that this next step would be a gift for both of us—some relief from the chaos and turmoil that we both struggled with. Somewhere along the way, we had drifted apart. I'm not sure if the isolation was intentional or if we withdrew because we had suddenly become incapable of rendering any solace to the other. Perhaps we had been hiding our own inner demise from one another, like a contagious burden that could not be exposed to any other life form for fear that it would spread.

We used to talk, at least. Through all the shit, we used to talk. Now, I was hoping to rekindle some of what we had lost. I knew her pride and maladjusted ego wouldn't allow her to reach out first, and I also knew my humor and ease of making others laugh would help her come around. This gesture of getting mutual tattoos was grander than the tattoos themselves—it was an affirmation that we had a bond stronger than life itself; that we were never alone. We had each other.

"Son of a—" I squirmed. "That fuckin' hurts!" I blurted out.

"Come on, suck it up. It's not that bad," she giggled.

"Seriously, that's probably the most painful tattoo I've gotten so far," I squinted.

Donny laughed and as fast as he began, he was finished. "You're all done here," he smiled as he wiped down my foot.

"Finally," I complained.

We placed our feet against one another's and looked down at the three stars: one pink, one blue and one green—our tattoos were a perfect match. She looked at me with a tear in her eye and smiled. "Thanks, sweetie. That was nice." She gave me a big hug.

"I love you, Mom." My heart swelled as I held my mother. Her scent was so familiar; it stirred up old feelings of the comfort I had found in her arms once upon a time. The little girl within me smiled. The woman I had become held her a little tighter. My mother—my best friend.

CHAPTER 13

"Mom, wake up. You're gonna be late for work!" I shouted from the kitchen. The coffee was percolating; the aroma danced around the kitchen as I stood in front of the machine watching it.

Drip, drip.

"Come on." I tapped my foot on the ground, waiting impatiently.

We both had to leave for work in thirty minutes. The only difference was I only had a two-minute car ride or a ten-minute walk, depending on which I chose. My mother, on the other hand, had a twenty-minute drive, which meant she was gonna be late for work regardless.

We had been living together for the last four months, and within that time, the roles had evidently been reversed. I was now the one with the responsible adult hat to wear; not that she had ever really worn it.

The burden was tiresome. I was a young professional who had to be on the ball. I wanted to prove myself and earn my place with the best. My mother still hadn't gotten out of her slump from her split with Malcolm.

Malcolm, on the other hand, had been doing amazing. I had gone to visit him at the bar a few times with my coworkers. He had lost the darkened circles that had cursed him for so many years. It pained me to think that my mother had caused another person physical ailment by being her difficult self, but I could no longer pretend that she wasn't who she was. There wasn't a doubt in my mind that she had the ability to become something more than the deliberately shattered woman persona she seemed to wallow incessantly in—but she needed to *want* to become something more, and I couldn't do that for her.

"Mom, come on!" I opened her door. The smell of booze swiftly invaded my nostrils with repugnant intensity.

She was still snoring. I walked around her bed and opened the curtains. The morning rays shone through the trees; it would be a beautiful day today.

"Mother, dammit, wake up. You're late for work!" I shouted at her.

She finally muttered, "Go to work, sweetie, I'm getting up."

"Coffee is made, have a good day," I said. I grabbed my coffee mug and left for work. I doubted she was going to get to work anytime before nine, but it wasn't my problem.

I had been driving back to the city on a regular basis to follow through with my appointments with

Paul. I hadn't felt the need to find a new therapist up here, seeing as I had a great connection with Paul. I knew that connection mattered more than a few hours' drive. I actually looked forward to our meetings now. The consistency and reliability I found in following through with my therapy was a predominant reason I had been faring so well.

***

"Allo, Miss Sophie," Madelaine greeted me. "Can I meet with you for a moment?" She gestured for me to enter her office.

"Of course," I said, following her.

Madelaine sat down at her desk and gestured for me to sit. "Listen Sophie, I don't want to waste your time. Your contract is coming to an end here. We have reviewed your work and are extremely satisfied with it. We don't currently have an opening in this unit, but we do have openings throughout the organization that I have recommended you for. I also suggest that you put your name in for a permanent position, which I do not doubt that you will receive." She smiled at me.

"Thank you, Madelaine. I haven't seen the time go by. I've had such a wonderful time working here; it's been a great experience. I will start looking at my options and will keep you posted. Thank you for the referral." I smiled at her and returned to my unit.

I really hadn't seen the time fly by. I sat down at my desk and pondered what I would do next. I had to make a decision soon and start applying for new positions within the next few weeks. What did I *want* to do? Now that was the question.

***

Hi Sophie, I'm calling in regards to the rent. Give me a call back. The voicemail had been left earlier that afternoon.

I wondered what could be up with the rent. I had been splitting it in half with my mother, which was a bargain even on her salary. I dialed back.

"Hey Sophie," our landlord answered.

"Hey, I just got your message. What's up?" I asked.

"Sophie, you guys are already two months behind. I don't know what to say, but I need you to pay those two months right away," he stated bluntly.

I nearly choked. "What do you mean, we're two months behind?" I could barely contain my disbelief. There had to be an error somewhere.

"It's quite simple. I haven't received any rent from you guys in the last two months. I can't let it drag on; it'll be worse. I'm sorry to put this on you but I've left messages on the house number and no one has returned my calls." He seemed annoyed.

"All right, I'm sorry about that. I'll look into it and you'll get your money by the end of the week, okay?" I scrambled to find a solution.

"For sure. Thanks, Sophie." He hung up.

"Fuck, Mom!" I blurted loudly.

There was only one logical reason behind this "missing" rent money, and I knew damned well what it was.

***

I was waiting for her when she got home from work.

"Hey Soph," she said as she flung her keys and purse on the counter.

"Hey Mom, I got a call today from the landlord," I began right away. "Care to fill me in as to why we are late on rent? Not just late, but two months behind?" I stared at her intently, awaiting an answer that couldn't undo what she had done.

"Umm, I'm pretty sure you didn't hand over your end of the rent, Sophie," she so easily stated.

I was flabbergasted. *How dare she accuse me of not paying up?* I had handed her the money in cash for her to pay him the full amount each month out of her account. I never once thought I would need to sign a piece of paper to prove I had handed the money over. My mouth was dry. I was in disbelief.

"Mom, are you fuckin' serious?!" I shouted. "You know damn well I gave you that money.

She turned her back to me and went to the fridge to retrieve a beer. Her nonchalant manner irritated me.

"Mom, we have to pay him two months of rent by the end of the week or he could evict us!" I was frantic.

"Listen, I don't know what happened to the money." She took a sip. "And I don't have the two months' rent in my account." She looked at me as though I were just some other bystander of her colossal debacle.

I bit my tongue. I was sickened by her lack of concern. This was my reputation; this was my new start at life. I had agreed that we should live together so we could help each other get on our feet—not knock the wind out of one another.

"You know what, I'll figure this shit out on my own. I can't have him talking about how we didn't pay him. He works in my field!" I shouted. "What happens here—in this house—affects me out there!" I vibrated with anger. "Did you ever once stop and think about me!?" I trembled. "Did you once stop and think about me, mother?!" I shouted at her again.

I hadn't screamed at her like this since I was a teenager.

She turned her back to me and placed her beer on the counter before resting her body against it as she hung her head.

"Calm down, we will figure it out," she said. "I will find the money and get it to the landlord. There's no need to panic." She glanced at me with her shame-ridden face. Her eyes pleading.

"No, Mom. It's done. I'll find a way to rectify this shit myself." I grabbed my jacket and went for a walk.

The breeze was chilly at that time of day; it swept up from the river in an incessant flow. One perk of living near a current was the rarity of mosquitos. I liked that. I inhaled deeply, embracing the freshness and releasing my tension. I placed my hands in my pockets. Under my fingertips I felt a pamphlet. I took it out of my pocket and opened it up:

Alcoholism: A Merry-Go-Round Named Denial.

It was from Al-Anon. How coincidental. A sign, maybe? I had never been one to believe in that type of thing, but the more I began to think about the procession of events, the more I noticed that I'd had signals along the way. I just had to open my eyes. I was finally, slowly, opening my eyes.

I opened the pamphlet, and of course, there was conveniently a meeting taking place the next day. As I stood there and shook my head, I decided it would probably be best if I attended.

***

The sconce lights illumined the entryway in a warm, subtle glow. The door had been left slightly open, so I let myself in. I walked down the hallway that had once appeared to house the dungeon of a serial killer . . . it now seemed peaceful and welcoming. It was a far cry from what I had envisioned last time. Bouquets lined the shelves that led to the meeting room. *Maybe they had redecorated?*

I entered silently and sat in the chair I had previously sat in. Most faces were familiar; a few others new. I reciprocated their smiles with a nod of my head, allowing myself to regain some of my composure. I hated talking in front of strangers, but I had been compelled to come. Tonight was the night I would share—if I could find solace in the simple action of sharing with people who understood, then I would leave here with more than I had come with.

Richard lead the group in prayer:

God, grant me the serenity to accept the things I cannot change, the courage to change the things I can, and the wisdom to know the difference. Amen.

"I'd like to take a moment on behalf of everyone here to say a warm welcome to the new faces, and to the not-so-new faces, that are gathered around this table. Please take a moment to praise yourself for having the courage to join us, and know that you are not alone," Richard opened.

"Now, the floor is open to anyone who wishes to speak. Please remember that everything that is shared in this space shall remain in this space. There are no judgments." He gestured for us to proceed.

I looked around quickly and cleared my throat before anyone could speak before me. It was now or never.

"I'd like to share," I heard myself say.

"Please, go ahead," Richard encouraged.

"I'm here because my mother is an alcoholic." I took a deep breath. The heaviness I had been carrying on my chest was burdensome. "I have spent my entire life trying to make excuses for her. I've lied for her, I've refused to acknowledge that she's lost control over her addiction, I've convinced myself that everyone around us was wrong . . ." I paused before continuing.

"But just a day ago I was faced with something different. It was the first time in my life that she tried to make me question my own integrity. And when she did that, I had this vivid flashback of my first day of kindergarten. I had been excited about going to school since I was told I was old enough to go. I wanted to be with my brother, you see, I wanted to see where he got to go every day while I stayed back with Mom and helped her at the bar. I admit that I was lucky in a way, because I used to get money for all those drawings I did for the regulars at the bar, but still, I wanted to go where Beau went." I paused for a moment, taking in a deep breath so I could continue.

"She had brushed my long, brown hair and bought me a brand-new outfit for my first day. I rarely had new clothes; everything I had ever gotten was a hand-me-down from my older cousins—curse and a blessing all at once. She sat me down on the washing machine and looked me over. She smiled. *Sophie, you are so very pretty, sweetie.* She caressed my hair. *You are just gonna love school, I know it.* She began tying my shoelace when Lucifer appeared—he walked in from the other room. I cringed at the sight of him. Why had she taken him back? She had promised—didn't she remember that she had promised us that he would never hurt any of us again? She had to remember.

"He came closer and began berating my mother for something I couldn't understand. She talked back, ignoring the fact that he'd placed himself right beside her. She continued to fix my shoes, when all of a sudden, he shouted, *look at me when I'm talking to you, bitch!* And that's when he pushed her. In that instant I saw her eyes enlarge, as she had been caught off-guard. She stumbled backward, in perfect projection to come into full contact with the corner of the counter. There was one thing—she had forgotten to let go of my shoelace." I continued.

"As she fell further, my body collided abruptly with the back of the washing machine. I slid down with a crash against the floor, but not before the back of my head got some of the blow. I wailed in pain and fear. My body ached. I trembled. She collided with the counter and immediately got back onto her knees and crawled to where I was.

"Sophie, sweetie. Are you hurt? she asked as she looked me over. Aside from a few red marks on my back, there were no other visible markings of the pain. I shook my head. I knew better than to prolong the attention that was set on me. He was still near. *I'm sorry sweetie, I'm so sorry. Let's get you going, okay? We don't want you to be late for the bus now.*

She picked me up and dusted me off, then rushed me out, anticipating the next attack. I looked her straight in her watery eyes, and for the first time, I felt betrayed by her. The feeling was so poignant it nearly stopped my heart. I had been betrayed. She had promised, *she had promised;* I had forgotten about that, until yesterday, that is.

"My brother took me by the hand and we ran out the door and all the way to the bus stop. She wasn't even there . . .

"So, in some ways, I've felt this exact way yesterday. Like that six-year-old." The tears streamed down my cheeks and my voice cracked with emotion, but I didn't care. I was too old now to allow her to have that much control over my existence. She was an adult, too, after all.

The box of tissues slid toward me. I took one and wiped the mascara away. I looked up to see that others had shed tears, as well. I believe that they cried for a pain they understood, for an incessant grief that tore us all up inside.

I felt my heart swelling with recognition and acceptance. I exhaled the weight of the world while these strangers held a sacred space of safety for me; the most unusual, but beautiful, experience.

Richard cleared his throat. "Thank you for sharing." He bowed his head.

I sat there and listened to the others share their stories, finding comfort and guidance in some aspects of their individual struggles. I was thankful I had given myself a chance; I was thankful I had come tonight—that I had created a strong support system. Maybe I would start rooting for myself from now on. *Maybe now I could consider myself brave.*

CHAPTER 14

"Mom, I have something I want to tell you," I said to her as I watched *Heartland* on CBC.

"What is it?" she replied.

"I've decided not to apply for a position over here," I began.

"Oh, okay. Where are you thinking of going?" she asked.

"Well, that's the thing. You know how I always said I wanted to go see those wide-open spaces one day?" I pointed to the image of the Rocky Mountains that passed on the screen.

"Umm, ya." She was listening.

"Well, I applied—for the fun of it—to this job Out West. I didn't think much of it, but they shortlisted me, gave me a phone interview, and gave me the job. Just like that." I tried to contain my excitement. I knew that the words would send a shock of disbelief through her.

She sat silently and took a sip of her beer. “Are you serious?” she finally asked.

I walked over and jumped up onto the counter to sit next to her. “Ya, Mom. I’m serious.” I sat silently, waiting for her to register the magnitude of what I was saying. There was no denying that the excitement I felt was palpable, but hanging above us loomed an ending. I had never been more than a few hours away from her. This would change *everything.*

“Oh my gosh, Sophie. That’s great. Really.” She hugged me. “I’m so proud of you. You always said you wanted to go Out West, now look at you go.” She smiled and caressed my check with her thumb. “When do you start?” she asked.

“Next month,” I answered.

As the words escaped my mouth, the reality of what I was doing began to sink in. In less than a month, I would leave everything I had ever known and embark on a journey to a place where I knew no one except for my estranged brother, whom I hadn’t seen in nearly a decade.

“Well, that sure is fast, sweetie. But you know I want what’s best for you and I know you can accomplish anything you put your mind to. I’m happy for you.” Her eyes filled with endearment and approval.

I could see that she truly was happy for me and believed in me. The mother who knew how to console me and was always my biggest fan had resurfaced from the fog. I was so happy to see her again. We had been so distant with one another this entire year that I didn’t think we would snap out of it;

I only wished our reunion would have occurred sooner than later.

I knew at that moment that I would miss her dearly.

***

"So, you talked to your brother?" she asked for the hundredth time.

"Yes, Ma. I did," I said, slightly annoyed, but touched that she was feeling just as edgy as I was.

"And you have everything that you wanted to bring with you packed into your car?" she questioned.

"Yes, Mother. I even have enough room to almost recline my seat so I can nap," I said sarcastically.

"I can't believe you're driving across the country all by yourself." She held me. "Your brother is going to be waiting for you when you get there, right?"

"Of course, Mom. He still has like four days to prepare for me. He already had his house all cleaned when he moved out, so its good to go." I smiled at her and gave her a kiss on the cheek.

I had spoken to my brother as soon as I received news that I got the position Out West. He had been living Out West for many years, and even had an empty house ready for me to move into. I was excited to see what the West looked like. I had dreamt of seeing the Rocky Mountains since I was a little girl. Knowing my brother was out there had enticed me to set a plan in action so I could finally find a way to build a relationship with him. I had been fucked up for too long; I wanted my brother to be a part of my next chapter. I had searched for many years to find a connection; maybe now that we were older, this was it. *This was our chance.*

I looked at my mother. Her beautiful eyes shimmered with the reflection of the light touching her tear. I held her tight and breathed her in as much as I could. Her scent had always guided me to find comfort within her reach. Now I knew that I wouldn't have the ability to find that comfort whenever I needed it. I tried to store as many details as I could of her face, her hair, her eyes, her dimples . . . and everything else that I could retain. Would my senses remember all these important things that I had held so dear my entire life? Would she forget *my* scent? Would she miss me as much as I would miss her?

I was unraveling. *Maybe this was a mistake. Maybe I shouldn't go; maybe I should just stay here. Maybe she will finally get some help and then we can move pass this. Maybe I can find a place to ease my restlessness and yearning to leave somewhere, and go somewhere not so far away.* I hated her at times, but I loved her. She was my best friend and my mother.

I was terrified.

"Sweetie." She took my face in her hands and looked into my eyes. Her heart understood what my mind was shouting.

"You, my girl, will succeed wherever you go. You were made for greatness. Do you hear me?" She peered into my eyes with the knowing intensity of a mother—*She was releasing me.*

I cried as I nodded. "Mom, maybe it's a mistake." The tears burned as they fell down my cheeks.

"I'm gonna be okay. You hear? I'm gonna miss you like hell, but I'm gonna be okay, I promise." She kissed me on the forehead as her tears streamed down her cheeks. She made her promise, and I believed her.

This would be the most difficult choice of my existence. Leaving her behind felt so wrong, but I would be lying if I didn't admit that I wanted—*needed*—to get away. I needed to find my path; to make something of myself on my own, just for a while.

"You go and make yourself rich," she teased, "so that when I turn fifty, I can retire and I can come Out West and you can take care of me," she joked.

I looked at her. "Ya, right Mom. I'll get right on it"

"That gives you a couple years to get yourself to where you need to go," she winked at me.

"Ok, I will," I sniffled.

"Stop your crying now. You can do this, sweetie." She held my face in her hands. "I am so proud of you. You are the best of me, you know that, right?" She kissed me.

I nodded. "I know, Mom."

"Go now, before you change your mind. Be safe and have a great adventure." She ushered me into my over-packed car.

"Okay." I took a deep breath. "I'm gonna miss you like crazy, Mom."

"Me too, sweetie. Me too." She swallowed back her tears.

I set my car in gear and slowly began driving away. I looked at her in my rear-view mirror; she waved frantically at me. I kept her in my sight for as long as possible until she ultimately vanished.

My tears blurred my vision and continued to pour down my cheeks as quickly as I wiped them away. "I can do this," I repeated to myself. "I can do this."

I turned the radio on and put in the compact disc I had made for the trip. Track number one came on:

over the speakers, the Dixie Chicks crooned the lyrics of "Wide Open Spaces."

I accelerated, feeling the wind cleanse my heart with every mile I drove. I cried, I screamed, I thought of turning back so many times I lost count . . . but at the end of the day, as I rested alone in my red, two-door Cobalt, I knew I was doing something just for me; I knew we'd all be all right.

EPILOGUE

"You know what? I'm just going to have to let her find her way. She's going to be fifty years old in a couple days—I can't keep protecting her."

As always, he listened to me without much more then a nod and a quiet *mmm*.

"I'm telling you, I think I'm finally letting go of my need to always help her out. If she really wants to move out here and be close to her children and her grandson, then she's going to have to get her act together," I stated firmly.

"I told her just like that—Mom, I'm super-excited that you want to come out here. Send me up your resume when you've completed it, and I will help you apply for some jobs, but I can't have you come out here without first getting a job. We can't afford an extra person, okay?"

"And what did she say?" he seemed slightly skeptical of the actuality and intensity of assertiveness I was claiming to have utilized.

I looked at him in defiance. "She said *of course.* Jesus, I love my mother, but I have a family of my own now. I really have to *let goooooo.*" I let the word roll off my tongue as though I were conjuring some spell.

I felt resolute; I felt like I had just grown up. Right there, I was no longer a little girl, and I was no longer a dysfunctional young woman. Okay, I still had a lot of shit to deal with, and I would probably continue to seek some professional help for many years to come, but in terms of actual progress, *this was it.* This had to count for progress, right? Paul had said it would take me a lot of hard work, and shit, I was working hard on working hard.

***

I called her again for her birthday a few days later.

"Happy birthdayyyyyyy, Mom. Happy, happy, happy birthday to you! Happy birthday to you, Happy birthday, dear Mommmmm, HAPPY BIRTHDAY TO YOUUUUU, OHHHH!" I sang in a lively fashion. "Can you believe it? The BIG Five-O?" My sing-song voice was an ear-sore, but it made her laugh.

"Ah jeez, Sophie, its just another day, sweetie. But thank you so much. I love you, sweetie."

"So, what are your plans for your special day? You are going to do something for yourself, right?" I asked.

"Its not a big deal, I'm just going to a friend's house, we're going to play some cards. I even get to see my best friend Chantal, so that's pretty neat. I don't want you to worry, sweetie, I'm not alone today." She had read my mind.

She still knew me so well. She knew that not being with her on her birthday shattered me. Since the day I was born, I hadn't missed her birthday—until I moved across the country, that is.

"I really wish I was there, Mom. I love you so much," I said, feeling remorse for my inability to celebrate with her or at least physically give her a hug.

"Listen, I'm about to run out of minutes. I'll go buy some and call you later. Thanks for the song, my girl. Talk soon, I love you!" she said, somewhat hurried.

"Okay, don't forget to call me back. Have a great time, Mom, be good! I love you."

She hung up with a *me too,* before I could add anything else.

***

That night, I sat in my rocking chair nursing my son. I looked at him and took in the purity of his little being. I questioned how I could possibly ever do anything to harm this incredible little being I had created. I vowed I would never let any harm come to him if I could prevent it. I knew I could be and would be completely available and prepared to be the type of mother he would need and deserve.

At least, I hoped I would.

I rocked him back and forth, back and forth, back and forth, singing to him for the thousandth time since his precious arrival— Frank Sinatra's "The Way You Look Tonight."

Some days, when I'm awfully low, and the world seems cold, I can feel a glow, just thinking of you, and the way you look, tonight . . .

I hummed the entirety of the song, over and over again, for an hour. When he was finally sleeping peacefully, I laid him down in his bed and felt the greatest luck to have him as my son.

"I love you, my love." I glanced down at him and cupped his tiny head. To think that not long ago, his entire body was the size of my hand.

I lingered a little longer, taking in the warmth of his little being. I finally pulled myself away and headed to our side of the room. I sat on the edge of my bed, feeling the weight of my fatigue. My body surrendered to the bed; I let myself fall gently onto my side and curled up into a little ball.

My eyelids were nearly closed when I saw Preston making his way up the stairs. He walked over to his dresser and removed his shirt, lifting it over his head. The muscles on his back contracted. He folded his day clothes and placed them on top of the dresser, neatly to the left corner. He passed his hands over his clothes, just like so. I watched him while he wasn't aware of my gaze upon him. His dark hair, perfectly trimmed and proper, his body meticulously cared for and nourished . . .

I flirted with the idea that maybe I loved him so much because of his meticulous, slightly rigid manners—his high expectations and dislike of spontaneity gave me a sense of security, a knowledge that he would always make the proper choices with regard to our well-being.

I knew I would always be safe with him.

He turned to me, suddenly quizzical and amused that he caught me staring. "So, she sounded good tonight?" He made his way to his side of the bed. As he sat down next to me, the weight of his body made the mattress sink toward him, thus compromising the comfortable position I had.

"Jeez!" I whined.

He stroked my back with the tips of his fingers. His warmth enveloped me—his touch comforting my mind. He didn't need to speak to *speak*. He was a man of few words; his touch was his grand form of communication.

I looked up at him. "Ya, she did. I'll talk to her tomorrow, I guess—she forgot to call back. I hope that means she's having a great time."

The worry in my voice was palpable. I couldn't help myself. I wished she would just be responsible and understand that her words should have worth. She should have known by now that I worried and that I would be waiting for her call.

I tried to make light of my response, but Preston had certainly picked up on the subtleties.

He pulled slightly away from me and stopped stroking my back. "Hey, where's that resolution you found just a few days ago? She's a grown woman. So are you. Don't worry so much. You worry too much." He shook his head in a disapproving manner.

He lay down beside me. His words caused me to question my actual resolution. I shrugged it off for now. I was exhausted. I pulled the blankets up to my neck as he settled in beside me.

"Ya, I guess you're right." I decided that an argument this late at night wasn't worth the energy.

Just this once, I would let it go. "Goodnight, babe. I need some sleep before our son wakes again."

I turned around to look at my phone one last time. It was ten-fifteen p.m. *She wouldn't be calling me now.*

I shut my phone off.

***

When I awoke, it was six-ten a.m.

I turned on my phone.

I had three new voicemails. *That can't be right.*

I sat up in my bed and pushed the play button; the voice of my cousin quickly came on the line. She sounded frantic.

Sophie, answer the phone. Sophie, its important.

Sophie, come on answer the phone.

Sophie, it's your mom. Listen, something happened. She had an accident. She's in the hospital in the intensive care unit. Sophie . . . I'm . . . I'm so sorry. It's not looking good. Call me back.

THE END

AFTERWORD

Dear reader, thank you.

You may relate to Sophies' journey— if you do, I want you to know that YOU MATTER.

Reach out for help! I know that sometimes it feels like there is no one there, but there is. Please find your support system. These people exist!

Listed below are a handful of helplines and organizations; both Canadian and American. May they offer some guidance.

Al-Anon/Alateen: www.al-anon.org

Alcoholics Anonymous: www.aa.org

Narcotics Anonymous: www.na.org

Crisis Text line Canada: text Talk to 686868 for English

text Texto to 686868 for French

Kids Help Phone Canada: www.kidshelpphone.ca

DAWN (DisAbled Women's Network Canada)

Domestic abuse helplines for across Canada: www.dawncanada.net/issues/crisis-hotlines/

United States National Suicide & Crisis Hotline: 1-800-784-2433

Teen Line USA: www.teenlineonline.org

The National Domestic Violence Hotline USA: www.thehotline.org

Reach out. Give yourself a chance. You are worth it. You matter. You are loved.

With all my love and gratitude,

ABOUT THE AUTHOR

Tanya Lee is still wearing an array of hats today. A mother of two amazing children, a Reiki Master Practitioner, and a seeker of the authentic self, she now embarks on a new journey as a first-time author. Although she is still wandering this world, not too certain where she stands, she now stands firmly (most of the time). She aspires to bring forth a greater sense of compassion and love into this world. Woven into her story, she hopes you hear the words: *you matter*.

Made in the USA
Middletown, DE
07 March 2019